This book
belongs to:

Aisha

To Mum and Fatti

Penny the Star

FABER-CASTELL

since 1761

Penny the Pencil has a proud heritage. She is made by the leading pencil manufacturer in the world, Faber-Castell. The Faber-Castell family have been making pencils for eight generations. It all started in a small workshop in Germany in 1761 and now the company employs 5,500 people worldwide. The company is run by Count Anton Wolfgang von Faber-Castell.

Faber-Castell is a company with great flair and vision. It is in the *Guinness Book of Records* for creating the world's tallest pencil at almost twenty metres high and has also made the most expensive pencil ever. The Grip 2001 pencil brings together these elements of design, quality and innovation. It has won many international awards. With its unique soft grip zone and comfortable triangular shape it has become a worldwide classic.

EILEEN O'HELY

Penny the Star

Illustrated by Nicky Phelan

MERCIER PRESS

WHAT YOU NEED TO READ

MERCIER PRESS
Douglas Village, Cork
www.mercierpress.ie

Trade enquiries to Columba Mercier Distribution,
55a Spruce Avenue, Stillorgan Industrial Park,
Blackrock, County Dublin

ISBN: 978 1 85635 542 1

10 9 8 7 6 5 4 3 2

Mercier Press receives financial assistance from
the Arts Council/An Chomhairle Ealaíon

Printed and bound by J. H. Haynes & Co. Ltd, Sparkford

Contents

Main Characters

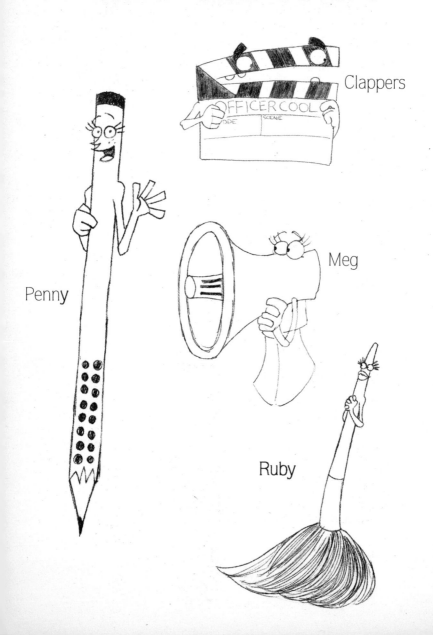

Clappers

Penny

Meg

Ruby

Bert

Ralph

Sarah

Smudge

Gloop

Black Texta

Polly

Chapter 1

Officer Cool

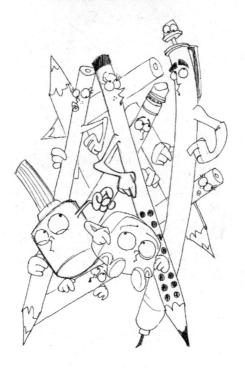

Inside a particular pencil case, inside
a particular little boy's school bag, the
pencils, rubbers, correction fluid and other
writing implements were having a very
bumpy ride.

'Wha-at's go-ing o-on?' asked Mack, a shiny, red mechanical pencil who looked decidedly seasick.

'I thi-ink Ra-alph's run-ning,' answered a grey lead pencil with bubbles on her skirt.

'Why-y?'

'May-be he-e's la-ate fo-or some-thing,' said the grey lead pencil, as she rolled into the bottle of correction fluid. 'Sor-ry Glo-op,' she apologised.

'Tha-at's o-kay, Pen-ny,' said Gloop, the bottle of correction fluid to the grey lead pencil. 'I ju-ust wi-ish Ra-alph wo-uld g-et the-ere so-on!'

There was a loud *thud!* and all the writing implements were slammed together.

'Ow!' said a little rubber, as Penny accidentally poked into it with her sharp point.

'Sorry, Smudge!' said Penny, pulling her toe out of the little rubber's belly button.

The writing implements wriggled around so they weren't jammed so tightly together. Just when they'd got comfortable the pencil case closed in around the middle.

'Ahhhhhhh … !' cried the writing implements as the pencil case was lifted into the air.

There was a loud zzzzzzzzipping sound and sunlight flooded the pencil case. A freckly hand poked through the zipper and started shuffling the pencils about. Penny rolled towards the hand. The thumb and forefinger closed around her and lifted her out of the pencil case.

Penny found herself in a small living-room. Her owner, Ralph, was seated at the dining table, pulling his homework out of his school bag. Next to him, Ralph's best friend, Sarah, was already hard at work. Sarah's pencil Polly, who looked identical to Penny, was skimming across the page, not even pausing for breath.

Once all his books were arranged, Ralph started writing. Ralph didn't write as fast as Sarah, which suited Penny, because it meant she had time to admire her own writing and have a good look around the classroom, or wherever Ralph happened to be. Today they were at Sarah's house, and Ralph seemed to be writing particularly slowly.

Penny looked up at Ralph, and noticed that he had one eye on his homework, and one eye on the big clock that was on the mantelpiece. As the minute hand ticked closer to four o'clock, Penny noticed that the amount of time Ralph spent looking at his homework grew smaller, and the amount of time he spent looking at the clock grew bigger.

At two minutes to four Ralph looked as though he was about to burst.

'Sarah,' said Ralph urgently, pulling on Sarah's sleeve.

'Not now, Ralph. You'll spoil my train of thought,' said Sarah, shrugging him off and continuing writing.

Just then Sarah's grandmother carried a tray with two glasses of orange juice and two large slices of freshly baked cake into the room.

'You two have been working so hard, I thought it was time you took a break,' she said, placing the tray on the coffee table in front of the television. 'Why don't you watch a little TV for a while? Is there anything good on at four o'clock?'

Sarah finally looked up from her homework.

'Is it four o'clock already? Why didn't you tell me, Ralph? It's time for *Officer Cool*!' said Sarah, leaping up from the table and running to turn on the television.

Ralph rolled his eyes, dropped Penny onto his open exercise book and ran to join Sarah in front of the television.

Penny peered carefully over the edge of the exercise book so she could see the

television. Sarah's pencil Polly, and some of
Ralph's other writing implements, rolled
over to join her.

Ralph's big, red dictionary shook his
head in disgust.

'Kids these days,' muttered Dictionary.
'All they want to do is watch television.
They'd find it far more educational to turn
off the box and pick up a good book!'

Dictionary turned to Ralph and Sarah's writing implements for agreement, but they all had their eyes glued to the television set. Dictionary shook his head, then turned to the television to see what all the fuss was about.

The theme music started and the words '*Officer Cool*' flashed up on the screen.

'What's this show about then?' asked Dictionary.

'*Officer Cool*, of course,' said Polly, distractedly.

A picture of a handsome man dressed in a police uniform appeared on the screen, along with the words: 'Starring Rick O'Shea'.

'Is that *Officer Cool*?' asked Dictionary.

'Yeah. He's the *co*-star,' whispered Penny, without taking her eyes from the television.

'The co-star?' exclaimed Dictionary. 'But the show's called *Officer Cool*. If this guy isn't the star, who is?'

All the girl pencils drew in their breath
as the camera zoomed in on Officer Cool's
shirt pocket. Poking out the top of it was a
very handsome pencil.

'That's him,' said Penny. 'Officer Lead'.

The credits finished and the show began.
Officer Cool was in a warehouse, walking
sideways with his back flat up against a
wall. Inside Officer Cool's pocket, Officer
Lead was pressed up tightly against Officer

Cool's chest. When Officer Cool got to the corner he peered around it carefully. From inside his pocket, Officer Lead did the same.

Just as the officers' heads poked around the corner, a shot rang out. Officer Cool ducked back behind the corner for safety and Officer Lead disappeared inside his pocket. Ralph, Sarah and all their writing implements drew in their breath.

The familiar 'Officer Cool is in hot pursuit' music played as Officer Cool took out his gun and gave chase. Ralph, Sarah and all their writing implements bopped along to the music as Officers Cool and Lead pursued the villain through the warehouse, down an alley, up a ladder and across rooftops. Even Dictionary, who was pretending not to like the show, found himself tapping his foot.

Finally Officer Cool gained on the villain and leaped at him. Both Officer Cool and the villain fell off the roof, and tumbled through a banner saying 'CONGRATULATIONS HOWARD AND EMMA' before crash-landing on a wedding cake. Officer Cool stood up, covered in cream, and pulled the cream-covered villain to his feet before handcuffing him.

The bridal couple and wedding guests gaped at them.

'Don't you just hate it when uninvited guests drop in?' said Officer Cool. 'I'll pay for the damage, of course.'

He reached into his shirt pocket and pulled out his cream-covered pencil and chequebook. Officer Lead licked the cream off his face and winked as Officer Cool wrote out the cheque.

'Isn't he just dreamy?' said Polly.

'Don't you mean creamy?' said Penny.
'What I wouldn't give to lick –'

'I could take him on,' said Mack,
bouncing backwards and forwards with his
fists up.

'Like you'd even get close!' snorted
Penny.

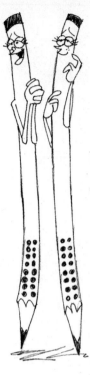

Mack stopped bouncing.

'You know,' said Amber, Ralph's orange pencil, 'they say that computers are taking over, but I'd like to see one of those overgrown calculators try to do even half the stuff Officer Lead can do!'

'Officer Lead is so cool,' said Penny. 'When I grow up I want to be a TV star just like him.'

'Now, now, Penny,' said Gloop. 'You've still got a lot of things to learn at school first. Your spelling is quite good …'

Dictionary nodded and smiled proudly.

'… but you still have a lot of work to do on history,' continued Gloop, 'and your geography is appalling. You still don't know whether Somalia is in Africa or Europe –'

'It's not my fault I'm incontinent,' said Penny. 'If Ralph ever bothered to do his geography homework I'd learn something. I don't think he's opened his atlas all year.'

'I'm not talking about Ralph,' said Gloop patiently. 'I'm talking about you –'

'Shhh! Ralph's coming!' warned Mack.

The writing implements resumed their positions on the open exercise book as Ralph and Sarah came back to the table to finish their homework. Ralph picked up Penny and began writing.

'You'll see, Gloop,' whispered Penny as Ralph paused to think. 'I'll be signing autographs one day. I can feel it.'

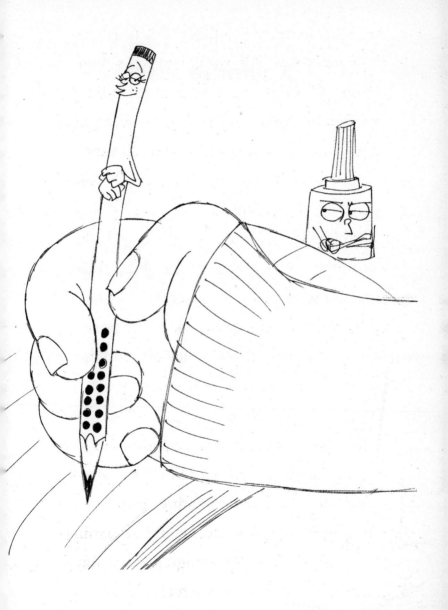

Chapter 2

A surprise guest

The chatter in the classroom at school the next day was all about *Officer Cool*. Mrs Sword, the teacher, had a very difficult time getting everyone to calm down enough to do their sums. However, the class settled down very quickly when Mrs Sword threatened to keep them in at playtime, and all the children were soon working quietly, with only the occasional whisper.

Having made sure that Mrs Sword wasn't looking, Ralph leaned over to Sarah and whispered, 'That was such a great episode of *Officer Cool* yesterday. Didn't you love the bit when they fell onto the wedding cake?'

'Rick O'Shea is so handsome,' said Sarah, her serious expression turning all dreamy. 'When I grow up, I'm going to marry him.'

'Sure, Sarah,' said Ralph, feeling just a little jealous. 'Like you'll ever meet him …'

'Ralph – if you have something so important to say that it can't wait until playtime, maybe you'd like to share it with all of us?' said Mrs Sword from the front of the classroom.

Ralph blushed and looked down at his book.

'Well? Stand up and tell everybody,' said Mrs Sword.

All the other children turned and looked at Ralph. Bert, the bully who sat behind Ralph and Sarah, sniggered.

Ralph stood up slowly and dropped Penny down on his exercise book.

The other writing implements poked

their heads out of the pencil case to see what was happening.

'Come on, then,' said Mrs Sword. 'What was so important that couldn't wait until the bell rang?'

'It's not really that important – ' began Ralph.

'Well it must be if you had to whisper it to Sarah during quiet time,' continued Mrs Sword. 'Especially when we have a special visitor coming today.'

Ralph looked down at the desk in embarrassment.

Mrs Sword folded her arms. Sarah looked at the clock nervously. It was not unknown for Mrs Sword to keep the whole class in after the bell if she felt like it, and she'd been threatening to do so all morning!

'We're all waiting, Ralph,' said Mrs Sword.

'Well, Sarah and I were just talking about *Officer Cool* –'

'Officer Cool!' chorused the children who sat closest to the door.

Ralph looked up in amazement as none other than Rick O'Shea, star of *Officer Cool*, strode into the classroom.

'Wow!' said Ralph.

'He's so handsome!' breathed Sarah.

'Hello, Aunty Pat,' said Rick O'Shea to Mrs Sword.

'Hello, Rick,' said Mrs Sword. 'Class, I'd like to introduce you to my nephew Rick. Most of you would know him as Officer Cool.'

The class sat wide-eyed and open-mouthed, hardly able to believe that Mrs Sword was related to their favourite television star.

While the class was distracted, Penny took the opportunity to roll over to Polly unnoticed.

'Look, Polly! It's Officer Cool. Do you think he's brought Officer Lead with him?'

All the writing implements poked their heads over Ralph and Sarah's pencil cases to take a look. There, in Rick O'Shea's shirt pocket, was none other than Officer Lead.

He winked at the coloured pencils, causing several of them to faint.

'It's really him,' squeaked Polly.

'*In the wood*,' said Penny.

'*In the wood*,' mimicked Mack, who was made of plastic. But none of the girl pencils were paying any attention to him.

'He's even more handsome in real life than he is on TV!'

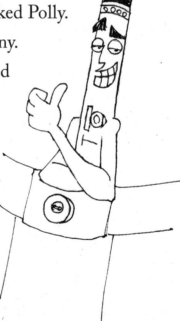

said Jade, Ralph's green coloured pencil.

'So, class, what do you say to our guest?' said Mrs Sword, who had never seen the children so gob-smacked.

'Good afternoon, Officer Cool,' chorused the class.

'Good afternoon, 2nd Class,' said Rick, chuckling. 'You can call me Rick.'

'Oh. We can call him Rick,' said Sarah, who was very excited to be calling an adult, especially a handsome, famous adult, by his first name.

'Would anybody like to ask Rick a question?' asked Mrs Sword.

The class erupted immediately into noise, as all the children tried to ask Rick several questions at once.

Rick looked around at the sea of eight-year-olds, unsure which question to answer first.

Seeing that her nephew was a little out of his depth, Mrs Sword clapped her hands until the room was quiet.

'One at a time!' said Mrs Sword. 'Rick will only answer your questions if you put your hands up –'

Thirty hands shot into the air.

Mrs Sword looked around the classroom and pointed at Ralph.

'Ralph, since you were just talking about *Officer Cool*, you may ask the first question,' said Mrs Sword, smiling.

Ralph couldn't believe it. One minute he was getting in trouble for talking about Officer Cool in class, and the next minute *Officer Cool* was in the room, and Ralph was allowed to ask the first question!

Ralph opened his mouth to speak, but only a little croak came out.

Mrs Sword, Rick, and the rest of the

class looked at Ralph expectantly.

'I think what Ralph wants to know,' said Sarah, coming to the rescue, 'is how did you become a TV star, Rick?'

Ralph smiled gratefully at Sarah. Sarah was also smiling, but at Rick rather than at Ralph. Ralph's smile turned to a frown.

Rick smiled back at Sarah. 'Acting may look easy, but it's actually a lot of hard work,' he said. 'As well as normal school, I went to acting classes, singing lessons …'

Gloop leaned towards Penny and winked at her.

'You see what I told you last night? School is important, even for television stars.'

But Penny was gazing at Officer Lead, and appeared not to hear Gloop.

'… and I spend two hours a day in the gym,' continued Rick, rolling up his sleeve and flexing his muscles.

Both the boys and the girls were very impressed with Rick's muscles. The boys rolled up their shirt sleeves and flexed their own, which were tiny in comparison.

Officer Lead, who was poking out of Rick's top pocket, also flexed his muscles. Penny, Polly and all the girl pencils ooh-ed and ahh-ed appreciatively. Mack flexed his muscles as well, but like the boys, Mack's muscles looked really tiny compared to Officer Lead, so he put his arms down quickly.

'Any other questions for Rick?' asked Mrs Sword.

Bert put his hand up.

'Bert. Your turn,' said Mrs Sword.

'Do they use real bullets in the guns?' asked Bert.

Rick and Mrs Sword both looked shocked.

'No, they don't, thank goodness,' said Rick.

Bert frowned and put his hand up again.

'And it's not real blood either,' Rick added hastily, guessing Bert's next question.

Bert looked disgusted.

'Moving right along,' said Mrs Sword pointing to the girl who sat behind Sarah. 'Lucy, do you have a question?'

'What about the cake in last night's episode?' asked Lucy. 'Was that real?'

'Unfortunately not,' said Rick laughing. 'It was shaving cream, and it tasted terrible!'

Mrs Sword noticed Rick glance at his watch.

'Now, Rick, I know you're in a hurry,' began Mrs Sword, 'but would you have time to sign a few autographs … ?'

Before Rick could answer, the whole class ran to the front of the room, carrying school books, pencil cases, and anything they could get their hands on for Rick to sign.

Rick took Officer Lead out of his pocket and started to sign his name on the nearest child's pencil case, but the pencil wouldn't write.

'That's odd,' said Rick, tossing Officer Lead into the bin. 'Does anybody have a pencil I could borrow?'

The children all ran back to their desks

in a mad dash to fetch Rick a pencil. Ralph seized Penny, who winked cheekily at Gloop.

'You see what I told *you* last night?'

Ralph was the first child back to the front of the classroom. He handed Penny to Rick.

'Ralph, wasn't it?' said Rick, signing the inside front cover of Ralph's geography book.

Ralph gaped in amazement. Rick O'Shea, star of *Officer Cool* and hero of all boys under ten, actually knew his name!

Rick handed the book back to Ralph. Ralph took the book in both hands and read, 'To Ralph from Rick. From one tough guy to another.' Ralph was so excited that he didn't even notice Rick had kept Penny to sign the next autograph.

The other children, including Sarah, pushed past Ralph to have Rick sign autographs for them. Sarah fought her way back through the crowd towards Ralph, waving her exercise book.

'Look, Ralph. Rick wrote 'Dear Sarah. All

the best. Love Rick.' *Love* Rick! Can you believe it?' said Sarah.

Ralph took his eyes off his own tough guy autograph to scowl at Sarah's love autograph.

'Has anyone missed out?' asked Mrs Sword.

The class all clasped their autographed items and shook their heads.

Absent-mindedly, Rick tucked Penny into his shirt pocket, where Officer Lead belonged.

Penny poked her head over the top of the pocket, looking even more excited than the children.

'In that case, we'd better let Rick get back to work,' said Mrs Sword. 'What do you say, class?'

'Thank you, Rick,' chorused the children.

'It was a pleasure,' said Rick. 'Keep watching *Officer Cool*, and er, keep doing your homework!'

As Rick walked out of the room, Penny climbed out of the pocket and waved at her friends over Rick's shoulder.

'She's really going to do it. She's really going to be a TV star!' said Amber, waving back.

The rest of Ralph and Sarah's writing implements smiled and waved at Penny.

Only Gloop looked a little concerned.

'And speaking of homework …' began Mrs Sword.

Just as Mrs Sword finished telling the children their homework the bell rang. The children packed up their books and pencils and filed out of the classroom, still excited about Rick's visit.

As Ralph and Sarah were walking out of the room, Mrs Sword said, 'Ralph, would you come and see me please?'

Ralph instantly forgot all about Rick's visit and remembered getting into trouble for talking.

'Since you wasted some of our class time today, I'm sure you won't mind making it up by emptying the bin?' said Mrs Sword.

'No, Mrs Sword,' said Ralph, picking up the bin and breathing a sigh of relief at the relatively light punishment.

Ralph carried the classroom bin to the large waste container in the corner of the playground. As he tipped the bin upside-down, he noticed something strange among the scraps of paper, apple cores, banana peels and scrunched up sandwich wrap. He put his hand into the rubbish and pulled out ... Rick O'Shea's pencil! Feeling very pleased with himself, Ralph stuffed the pencil into his shirt pocket so he could be just like Officer Cool.

Chapter 3

Lights, camera ...

Penny couldn't believe her luck. Just last night she'd told everyone her plans to become a TV star and today it was really happening. And in such a high-profile show like *Officer Cool*! Penny peered out eagerly from Rick's shirt pocket as he drove to the television studio. Rick showed his pass at the gates of Cool TV, and parked outside a trailer with a big, gold star on it.

Rick got out of the car and went up the steps to the trailer door. As Rick opened the door, Penny noticed a little star in the middle of Rick's star saying 'Officer Lead'.

'I'll have to get that changed to Penny!' thought Penny to herself.

Inside, Rick's trailer was just as glamorous as Penny had imagined. There was a mirror with bulbs all around it. In front of the mirror was a bench that was covered in make-up and hair-styling equipment. There was a silver bucket filled with ice and a bottle of champagne, piles of fan mail, a chair with another gold star saying 'Rick', and dozens of people rushing around holding make-up palettes, curling wands and costumes.

A woman with extremely boofy hair and very thick make-up was holding a make-up palette and a make-up brush.

'Rick, honey, where have you been?' asked the woman, smiling at Rick and bustling him into a chair in front of the mirror. She tied a hairdresser's cape around Rick's neck.

Penny wriggled her way up Rick's chest and poked her head out of the collar of the cape so that she could see.

'Sorry, Shanna. I promised my aunt I'd visit her primary school class …' began Rick.

'Don't apologise to me,' said Shanna. 'Mr Wolf is going crazy looking for you –'

The trailer door burst open and a short, grey-haired man wearing a khaki photographer's vest stormed in. A

megaphone was dangling from his pudgy
hand.

'O'Shea. Delighted you could fit us into
your busy schedule. We've been waiting on
set for more than an hour,' said the man
sarcastically.

'I'm sorry, Mr Wolf,' said Rick a little tersely. 'I went to visit my aunt's primary school class –'

'Save your sob stories for the ladies,' continued Mr Wolf. 'I'm not interested in your lame excuses. You stars are all the same. Think you can waltz in here whenever you like, the rest of us waiting on you hand and foot ...'

Mr Wolf looked Rick up and down. Not only Shanna, but a whole team of people were busy attending to Rick's make-up, hair and fingernails, and polishing his shoes.

'... well it's just not on. You're treading a thin line, O'Shea. I want you on set ...' continued Mr Wolf, putting the megaphone up to his lips and yelling through it, '... IN FIVE MINUTES!'

Mr Wolf turned on his heel and left, slamming the door behind him.

All the costume ladies paused.

'You heard him, ladies. Five minutes,' said Shanna. 'Let's get to work!'

The costume ladies began working on Rick again, brushes, nail files and powder-puffs flying feverishly.

Penny watched as Shanna put blusher on Rick's cheeks. She didn't notice the curious pair of eyes on her until the make-up brush said, 'You're not Rick's usual pencil. What are you doing here?'

Penny looked at the make-up brush in surprise. Until that moment she never thought that everyday objects could talk.

'Oh, I'm Penny. I'm actually Ralph's pencil –' began Penny.

The make-up brush continued quizzing Penny as she applied make-up to Rick's face.

'Who's Ralph? The new best boy?' asked the make-up brush.

Penny looked puzzled.

'He might be the best boy. Rick did sign his autograph first …'

'Uh-huh,' said the make-up brush. 'So what are you doing here?'

'Well, when Rick was signing autographs for Ralph's class –' began Penny.

'Is that why he was late?' interrupted the make-up brush.

'I suppose so –' said

Penny doubtfully, finding it hard to keep track of what was going on. Watching the make-up brush move backwards and forwards, and dealing with her constant interruptions was making Penny feel all dizzy and confused.

'Well go on,' said the make-up brush.

'Er … right. Where was I?' asked Penny.

'Signing autographs,' prompted the make-up brush.

'Yes. Rick pulled out Officer Lead –' began Penny.

'Officer Lead?'

'You know, the pencil Officer Cool always writes parking tickets with –'

'Oh, you mean Barney,' said the make-up brush.

'Whoever. Anyway, Officer Le – Barney wouldn't write –'

'Of course he wouldn't write. He's a

prop,' said the make-up brush.

'A prop?' asked Penny. She'd never heard the word 'prop' before.

'Something that looks good on stage, but when it comes down to it, it's only shooting blanks. A bit like Herbert here,' explained the make-up brush, gesturing to Rick's gun, Herbert, who was lying on the bench.

At the sound of his name, Herbert looked around wearily, then lay down again and went back to sleep.

53

'Oh. Well, anyway,' continued Penny, 'Barney didn't write, so Ralph gave me to Rick, and I signed autographs for everyone. Then, when it was time to go, Rick put me in his pocket and brought me here.'

'I see,' said the make-up brush, pausing to look at Rick's face critically. 'That's enough rouge, I think.'

The make-up brush turned her attention back to Penny.

'So if you're here and Barney isn't, I guess that means you're going on set now?' the make-up brush asked Penny.

'I guess so!' said Penny, getting very excited as Shanna removed Rick's make-up cape.

As Shanna put the make-up brush in the jar, it called out to Penny, 'Learned your lines?'

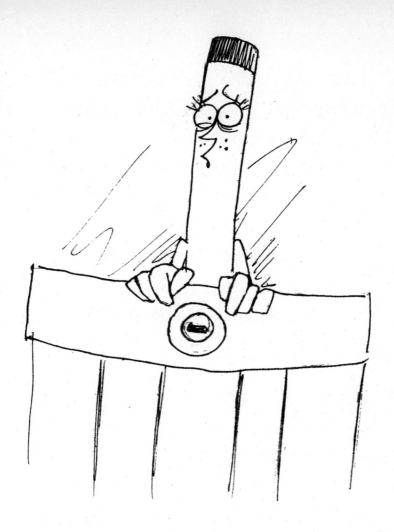

'What lines?' cried Penny in a panic, as
Rick got up to leave the trailer.

Chapter 4

... **Action**

Penny panicked the whole way across the parking lot from Rick's trailer to the studio. 'My lines? Does Officer Lead normally have lines?' Penny asked herself, racking her brain.

Rick threw open the door to the studio and Penny was greeted with another amazing sight. She was actually inside Officer Cool's police station. But unlike on television, it only had three walls.

Where the fourth wall should have been there were several large cameras on very wide, movable bases. There was a long, fluffy microphone hovering above the set and several big spotlights making the dark, indoor studio sparkle like it was outdoors on a bright, sunny day. The floor just outside the police station was strewn with oodles of cables. And sitting in the middle of everything on a director's chair was Mr Wolf.

Mr Wolf was barking orders at everybody through his megaphone. When he saw Rick, he looked at his watch pointedly and said, 'Okay people. It looks like our star has decided to grace us with his presence. Places everybody.'

Rick walked calmly to the edge of the set, just out of shot of one of the cameras.

A boy held a clapperboard in front of the camera. It seemed to Penny that, like the make-up brush, the clapperboard was alive, but asleep and snoring gentling.

Mr Wolf raised the megaphone to his lips.

'Aaaaaaaaaaand … action!'

'Episode 304. Scene 27. Take 1,' said the clapperboy, slamming the top down on the clapperboard.

The clapperboard's eyes flew open and he clenched his fists.

'Hey!' yelled the clapperboard. 'How would you like it if someone came up to you while you were sleeping and rammed your teeth together?'

To Penny's surprise, neither the clapperboy, nor any of the other humans, noticed what the clapperboard had said, and filming began.

Rick strolled briskly across the set.

'Cut!' cried Mr Wolf.

'What was wrong with that?' asked Rick.

'Too fast,' said Mr Wolf. 'Do it again. Places people. Aaaaaaaaaaand … action!'

The clapperboard, who had fallen asleep again and was snoozing quietly was brought up in front of the camera again.

'Episode 304. Scene 27. Take 2,' said the clapperboy, slamming the top down on the clapperboard.

The clapperboard's eyes flew open a second time and he waved his fists at the clapperboy.

'You do that again and I'll …'

Rick walked across the set again.

'Cut!' called Mr Wolf through the megaphone.

Rick spun around and faced the director.

'Too slow,' said Mr Wolf dismissively.

The clapperboy brought the clapperboard up to the camera a third time. This time the clapperboard was awake, his eyes darting from where the clapperboy's hands were holding him on either side of his tummy.

'Don't you even think about it …' warned the clapperboard.

'Aaaaaaaaaaand … action!' said Mr Wolf.

'Episode 304. Scene 27. Take 3,' said the clapperboy, slamming the clapperboard's top down again.

'Why you little …' said the clapperboard as the clapperboy laid him down again.

Rick took two steps onto the set.

'Cut!' cried Mr Wolf.

The clapperboy brought the clapperboard up in front of the camera again. This time the clapperboard was sporting a black eye.

'Oh yeah? You want a piece of me?' he challenged.

'Episode 304. Scene 27. Take 8,' said the clapperboy, slamming the clapperboard together again.

'Ouch! That was a rough one,' murmured the clapperboard.

'Cut!' cried Mr Wolf.

The clapperboard was brought up

again with a fat lip.

'I'm warning you ...' he said.

'Episode 304. Scene 27. Take 12,'
said the clapperboy, slamming the
clapperboard's mouth tightly shut again.

'Cut!' cried Mr Wolf.

The actors took their places again and
Mr Wolf gave the signal. The clapperboy
brought the poor clapperboard up to the
camera again. He had bandages and grazes
all over him.

'Go on, try it, just try it ...' said the
clapperboard weakly.

'Episode 304. Scene 27. Take 17,'
said the clapperboy, slamming the
clapperboard's head down again.

'I can't feel my legs ...' squeaked the
clapperboard.

After several more takes, filming ended
for the day.

'Okay people. That's it for today,' said Mr Wolf. 'Go home. Learn your lines. Practise walking. We've got an early start in the morning on location. Don't be late.'

The cast and crew filed out of the studio. Rick went back to his trailer and slammed the door. He took off his police shirt (with Penny still in the pocket) and laid it on the bench next to the jar containing beauty applicators, including the make-up brush Penny had been talking to earlier. Once he was fully changed, Rick left the trailer, slamming the door a second time.

'Hey, Penny. You in there?' called the make-up brush. 'It's safe to come out now. Rick has left the building.'

Penny crawled out of

the shirt pocket and looked
around. She saw the make-up
brush looking down at
her.

'How was
your first day
on the set?' asked
the make-up brush.
'Did you remember all your lines?'

Penny shook her head in
disappointment.

'I didn't get to do anything,' said Penny.
'All that happened was Rick walked up and
down a few times, the director kept calling
"CUT", and this flat black and white guy
got a lot more camera time than I did –'

'You think I enjoyed that?' said a familiar
voice over by the door.

Penny and the make-up brush looked
towards the door. The clapperboard was

squeezing his way through the gap at the bottom. He wriggled to an upright position and dusted himself down with his pudgy little fingers.

'That was hard work today,' he said.

'Let's have a look at you, Clappers,' said the make-up brush to the clapperboard.

The make-up brush leaped over the edge of the jar and onto the bench next to Penny in one graceful movement. She then took a deep breath and jumped onto the floor, her

bristles making a nice parachute.

Penny tried to copy, but her toe got caught up in the folds of Rick's shirt. She tumbled onto the floor, landing with a painful bump.

Not noticing Penny's mishap, the make-up brush hopped across to Clappers. She read the scrawled writing on his front.

'Take 58? Mr Wolf made Rick do the scene 58 times?' asked the make-up brush.

'Lucky the guy wrote that on my front, otherwise I would have forgotten that he'd slammed my head into my body 58 times,' said Clappers angrily.

'There, there,' soothed the make-up brush. 'We'll have you looking like new in no time.'

'Thanks, Ruby,' said Clappers.

Ruby the make-up brush dabbed gently at Clappers as though she were applying make-up. Penny couldn't see exactly what

Ruby was doing because the cloud of pinkish dust from Ruby's bristles acted like a smoke screen. Once the dust had settled, Penny was amazed to see Clappers looking as good as new. Ruby stepped back to admire him.

'All better,' said Ruby. 'You scrub up quite handsome.'

'Well, I do spend a lot of time in front of the camera,' admitted Clappers modestly.

'Have you met Rick's new co-star, Clappers?' asked Ruby.

'We haven't been formally introduced,' said Clappers, putting out a hand. 'I'm Clappers.'

'I'm Penny,' said Penny, shaking Clappers' hand carefully, in case he was still injured.

Clappers looked Penny up and down.

'You don't look much like Barney,' he said doubtfully.

'Well I wouldn't, would I?' said Penny. 'Barney's a prop while I'm a real pencil.'

'A real pencil, eh?' said Clappers. Leaning towards Ruby he muttered; 'Does wardrobe know about this? What if she makes a stain?'

Penny's ears pricked up. 'Don't worry. I won't make any stains. I only write on paper, and the occasional pencil case.'

'I wish I could say the same for the black texta ...' began Clappers, chuckling. At the mention of 'black texta' Penny turned white.

'... that scribbles all over my front ...'

As Clappers kept talking, Ruby noticed that Penny had grown quiet.

'Penny? Are you all right?' asked Ruby.

Penny looked at Ruby and forced a smile.

'I'm fine,' said Penny.

'Are you sure? You're looking a bit peaky. I know what you need ...'

Ruby hopped towards Penny and dabbed at her. A pinkish powder filled the air, and Penny couldn't see anything.

After a few moments Ruby hopped back. As the dust settled Ruby drew in her breath.

'You look gorgeous!' said Ruby. 'Come take a look at yourself. Clappers?'

Clappers waddled over to Ruby, who climbed on top of him.

'Ready?' asked Clappers.

Ruby nodded.

'One ... Two ... Three!' said Clappers.

Clappers flung his mouth open and Ruby soared back up onto the shelf in front of the mirror. She beckoned for Penny to follow.

'Are you sure it's safe?' asked Penny.

'Of course it's safe,' said Clappers. 'You

just saw how easy it was. Hop on!'

Nervously Penny climbed aboard Clappers.

'Here we go,' said Clappers. 'One … Two … Three!'

Clappers flung his mouth open and Penny sailed towards the bench. But unlike Ruby's smooth flight, Penny twisted and turned in mid-air before crashing into the mirror and sliding down to the bench.

Penny picked herself up and looked in the mirror. She was not impressed with her reflection.

'Hang on a minute!' said Ruby.

Ruby gave Penny a quick, powdery touch-up.

'There. Take a peak now,' said Ruby.

As the powder cleared, Penny found herself face to face with her immaculate reflection.

'Oh, wow!' she said. 'I look like a star.'

'Yeah, but looks aren't everything,' said Clappers, turning himself upside-down so he was balanced on his head.

'One … Two … Threeeeeeeeeeeeeeeeeeee!' said Clappers, opening his mouth wide and flying through the air before landing neatly on the bench.

'Take it from me, kid …' said Clappers, as Ruby rolled her eyes, 'I spend a lot of time in front of the camera, and it ain't as easy as it looks. By the way, Ruby, marvellous make-up job!'

Ruby nodded her head at the compliment. Penny was staring at Clappers, waiting to hear his pearls of wisdom about acting.

'The most important thing is deportment,' said Clappers.

'De-what-ment?' asked Penny. She was usually good with words, but having

crashed into the mirror she was feeling a
bit dizzy and out of sorts.

'Deportment,' repeated Clappers. 'The
way you stand and move around. Pretend
there's a piece of string going through your
body from your head to your toe.'

'Like my lead?' suggested Penny.

Clappers exhaled with forced patience.

'No. Like a piece of string,' he said. 'It's coming out of the top of your head, making you stand up straight and tall. Pull in your stomach.'

Penny breathed in and sucked in her stomach.

'Puff out your chest,' ordered Clappers.

Penny puffed out her chest as far as she could.

'Good. Now suck in your cheeks.'

Penny sucked in her cheeks until she looked like a fish.

'Not those cheeks,' said Clappers, rolling his eyes.

'Which other cheeks?' asked Penny, through fishy lips.

Ruby leaned over and whispered in Penny's ear.

Penny's eyes widened in surprise.

Penny sucked in her 'other' cheeks and teetered precariously on her toe.

'Now, you're playing a police pencil,' said Clappers, 'so you have to look authoritative. Try frowning a little.'

Penny frowned a little.

'More,' said Clappers.

Penny furrowed her brow harder until she looked quite aggressive.

'Not that much,' said Clappers.

Penny relaxed her face muscles slightly.

'That's it. Good,' said Clappers. 'Now, eyes up, and walk!'

Penny, feeling most uncomfortable, took two hops before tripping and falling flat on her face. Ruby ran to her aid.

'It's going to be a long night,' said Clappers, shaking his head.

Chapter 5

On location

After a long night of acting lessons, Penny awoke feeling strangely refreshed for her first day filming on location. She felt like she'd spent the night having a nice, all-over massage instead of prancing up and down with her cheeks sucked in.

'That rumbling woke me up at about five o'clock,' whinged Wanda the curling wand while she was plugged in and warming up.

'What rumbling?' asked Penny.

'Didn't you hear it?' asked Ruby.

'No,' said Penny. 'Was it a thunderstorm?'

'You'll see when you go outside,' said Ruby mysteriously, as she touched up Penny's make-up.

The door opened, and Penny and the beauty applicators all lay down immediately.

Penny waited impatiently while Rick had his make-up done, anxious to see what had happened outside while she'd been sleeping. Finally Rick picked Penny up, put her in the pocket of his Officer Cool costume and opened the trailer door.

Penny couldn't
believe it. They were
no longer in the car
park of Cool TV,
but in the most
magnificent street
in the world!
The cars were
all so shiny they
sparkled, and they
were parked outside a big, old-fashioned
building. The building had huge pillars
along the front and over twenty stairs
leading up to big wooden doors with brass
handles and a big sign saying 'City Bank'.

All the cameras and spotlights and
cables from the studio yesterday were in
the middle of the street outside the bank,
with Mr Wolf's director's chair, naturally,
right in the middle.

To Penny's delight, Rick walked towards the building. He walked right up the stairs and opened the door. Penny took a deep breath, imagining what the inside of the bank would look like. She was quite surprised.

The door was made of cardboard, not wood, and instead of leading into a building it opened on to grass, trees and a little duck pond. Penny perked up when she recognised it as the park that Ralph and Sarah sometimes had picnics in over the summer holidays.

Just the other side of the door a man was busy pinning a big picture of the inside of a bank across the doorframe.

'Step away, please. Step away,' said the man, shouldering Rick out of the way with a friendly nudge.

'Not finished yet, Rob?' asked Rick,

purposefully standing in the man's way and
winking.

'I would be if the talent would get out of
the way,' said Rob. 'Do us a favour and hold
these,' he continued, passing Rick a box of
tacks.

'Five minutes!' cried Mr Wolf through

his megaphone, as everybody scampered around frantically, making the finishing touches to the set.

'This looks really good. Really lifelike,' said Rick, complimenting Rob's set-building as he held a tack in place for him.

'Something in front of the camera has to look good,' added Rob, missing the tack and accidentally hitting Rick's thumb with his hammer.

'That hurt!' said Rick.

'Places people!' cried Mr Wolf through the megaphone.

Rick walked over to a parking meter in front of the bank. The little flag on the parking meter said 'expired'. Rick took out his notebook, and then pulled Penny out of his pocket, ready to write a parking ticket. Penny sucked in her cheeks, puffed out her chest, and put on her biggest smile for the cameras.

When everybody was in position, Mr Wolf put the megaphone up to his lips and said, 'Aaaaaaaaaaand … action!'

The clapperboy brought Clappers up to the camera. After the long night of teaching Penny how to act, Clappers had fallen fast asleep. The clapperboy prised Clappers' mouth open and said, 'Episode 304. Scene 32. Take 1,' before slamming Clappers' mouth shut.

Clappers woke up and looked around in alarm.

'Who did …? What was …? Huh …?' spluttered Clappers.

Trying to stifle a giggle, Penny pulled a straight face and started to write the parking ticket when an alarm sounded. Rick looked up as a masked bandit in a black-and-white striped top, carrying a bulging cloth bag with a dollar symbol on it, ran down the stairs of the bank, bank notes flying out of the money bag.

Rick put Penny in his pocket, pulled Herbert the gun out of his holster, and gave chase.

'Cut!' cried Mr Wolf, getting out of his chair

and storming towards Rick.

'What did I do wrong that time?' asked Rick, quite exasperated.

Mr Wolf reached into Rick's shirt pocket and pulled out Penny.

'What. Is. This?' said Mr Wolf through clenched teeth, struggling to control his temper.

Penny shied away from Mr Wolf.

'It's. A. Pencil,' said Rick calmly, imitating Mr Wolf.

'I can see that, O'Shea. What happened to the prop you were using yesterday?' demanded Mr Wolf.

'I must have left it in the trailer. I'll go look,' said Rick, turning to walk off-set.

'No you won't,' said Mr Wolf. 'You'll stay right where you are. Do I need to remind you that we're on a tight schedule? Shanna – do something with this pencil.'

Mr Wolf held Penny by only two fingers in his outstretched arm. Penny dangled dangerously over the hard asphalt below.

Shanna took Penny safely in all four fingers and looked at her quizzically.

'Try and get it looking at least a little like the one O'Shea lost yesterday,' said Mr Wolf in a bored tone. 'Otherwise the continuity boys will have a field day.'

Mr Wolf stalked back to his chair.

Shanna reached behind her back. Penny watched curiously as she pulled out …

'Ruby!' said Penny. 'I didn't know you were allowed on set.'

'There's a lot of things you don't know about show business yet, honey. Now hold still. I have to make you look all policeman-like.'

With a flourish of movement and a lot of pink powder, Ruby dabbed at Penny before taking a step back and waiting for the powder to settle.

'That should do,' said Ruby, as she found herself face to face with a very professional, no-nonsense-looking Penny.

'Now get in there and nail that scene!' said Ruby, winking.

Penny nodded as Shanna passed her back to Rick.

'Ready to roll,' said Mr Wolf. 'Aaaaaaaaaaand … action!'

The clapperboy held Clappers in front of the camera and said, 'Episode 304. Scene 32. Take 2.'

He rammed Clappers' mouth shut, while Clappers could do nothing except give him an evil stare.

Rick pretended to write the parking ticket when the alarm rang a second time. Just like before, the masked bandit carrying

the bulging cloth
bag ran down the
stairs of the bank,
with bank notes
flying everywhere.
Rick pocketed
Penny, pulled out
Herbert the gun,
and leaped on the
bonnet of the car to give chase. The 'Officer
Cool's in hot pursuit' music started playing.
Penny started to bop along to the music
as usual, then remembered that she was
supposed to be a serious police pencil. She
did her best impression of Officer Lead's
crime-fighter face as Officer Cool chased
the bank robber.

As usual, Officer Cool gained on the
bank robber and leaped at him, and both
came crashing to the ground. With his foot

in the middle of the bank robber's back, Officer Cool handcuffed him and picked up the empty money bag. He dangled it in front of the bank robber's eyes and said, 'That just goes to show. Crime doesn't pay.'

'Cut!' cried Mr Wolf through the megaphone. 'That's a wrap, people. Don't forget to pick up your script for the next episode …'

Mr Wolf put the megaphone down and murmured, '… that's if there *is* a next episode.'

Hearing Mr Wolf's little mutter, the megaphone opened its eyes wide in alarm.

*

Back in Rick's trailer, Ruby and the other beauty applicators gathered around Penny, chatting excitedly.

'You did really well today, Penny,' said Ruby.

'You made her look really authoritative, Rube,' said Wanda.

'Ladies. If I could have your attention,' said Clappers. His voice was very loud and strange, with a kind of buzzing sound.

Penny and the beauty applicators turned around to look.

Clappers was standing in the doorway, holding Mr Wolf's megaphone up to his lips.

'Meg has something important to tell us,' said Clappers.

He placed Meg the megaphone on the ground and smiled at her encouragingly.

'The show's in trouble,' said Meg, in a voice so quiet, Penny and the beauty applicators could barely hear her.

'What?' said Ruby loudly, sticking a finger in her ear to clean out the wax.

'I said,' said Meg, a teensy bit louder, 'the show's in trouble.'

A chorus of 'what's' and 'why's' erupted from the beauty applicators, which was drowned out by Penny whining, 'But I only just started!'

'Don't worry Penny,' said Clappers. 'It's nothing to do with you. Meg, tell the others what you told me just now.'

Meg cleared her throat.

'Well …' she began softly.

The others all gathered in a tight semi-circle to hear her.

'… Just after Mr Wolf told everybody to pick up their script for the next episode, I heard him say "that's if there is a next episode",' said Meg.

'What do you think he could've meant by that?' asked Wanda.

'It means the studio might be giving

Officer Cool the chop,' said Clappers.

'But they can't do that,' said Penny, more outraged than all the others put together. '*Officer Cool* is Ralph's favourite TV show! All the kids in his class at school love it.'

'Do you know why they're canning the show, Meg?' asked Ruby.

'Something to do with ratings,' continued Meg. 'I overheard the producer talking to Mr Wolf and he said that not enough children are watching the show so none of the toy companies are paying to advertise.'

'That's not true!' said Penny. 'All the children in Ralph's class watch *Officer Cool*. They can't take it off the air.'

The other implements all muttered in agreement.

'No one said that they're taking *Officer Cool* off the air,' said Meg, just loudly enough to be heard over the muttering.

'But didn't you just say they weren't going to make any new episodes?' asked Ruby.

'I did,' said Meg. 'But that doesn't mean that they won't show re-runs.'

Everybody gasped. All the beauty applicators were horrified.

Penny looked around nervously.

'What's a re-run?' she asked.

The others all shook their heads in a friendly yet I-can't-believe-you're-so-stupid manner.

'Re-runs are when they stop making new episodes of a show and just replay the old ones,' said Clappers.

'But that's terrible!' said Penny. 'Ralph has already seen all the old episodes. He'll be bored.'

Ruby put her hand on Penny's arm and said, 'It's even worse than that.'

Penny's eyes widened in alarm.

'What could be worse than Ralph being unhappy?' asked Penny in a small voice.

'We'll all be out of a job,' said Ruby.

Penny gasped.

'Unless ...' began Clappers.

'Unless what?' said Penny.

Everyone turned to Clappers, who was staring into space with the beginnings of a grin, as an idea occurred to him.

'Unless someone in front of the camera gives them a reason to keep making new episodes,' said Clappers.

Everyone turned to Penny.

'He's right, honey,' said Ruby. 'You're the one the producer sees, so he's going to be watching you closely. It's all up to you now.'

Penny looked at the concerned faces around her. She smiled weakly and gave a nervous little titter.

Chapter 6

An undesirable audience

While everything was going topsy-turvy
for Penny, life was going on as usual
for Ralph. Sarah's granny was at the
hairdresser's having another blue rinse put
in, so Sarah had come over after school,
and they were both sitting at the table
doing their homework with the television

on in the background.

Ralph rifled through his pencil case, making lots of noise and causing Sarah to look up in exasperation.

'Sarah, have you seen my pencil?' Ralph asked.

'You haven't lost it again, have you?' said Sarah.

'No …' said Ralph, feeling foolish. 'Maybe I could just check in your pencil case … To see if you've picked it up by mistake?'

Sarah rolled her eyes and tipped the entire contents of her pencil case out on the table.

'Honestly, Ralph, you'd lose your head if it wasn't screwed on,' said Sarah.

From the television in the corner, the *Officer Cool* theme music started, and Ralph abandoned his search.

'Ooh. It's time for *Officer Cool*!' said Ralph.

Ralph and Sarah leaped up from the table and sprinted to sit on the floor in front of the television. All Ralph and Sarah's writing implements arranged themselves eagerly on the table to watch with more enthusiasm than usual, because they knew that today would be Penny's first television appearance.

After the theme music ended, the first scene opened with Officer Cool sitting at his desk in police headquarters, writing something. The camera zoomed in on the pencil in his hand as Officer Cool signed the paper with a flourish, saying, 'And that, my friend, is the letter of the law.'

Penny, dressed as a police officer, winked at the camera.

All Ralph and Sarah's writing implements clapped and cheered.

'Isn't she doing brilliantly?' said Amber.

'Who would have thought our little Penny would grow up to be such a big star?' remarked Jade.

'What do you think, Gloop?' asked Polly quietly, noticing that Gloop was frowning slightly.

'There's no doubt that Penny's doing remarkably well, and I'm very proud of her.

It's just …' trailed off Gloop.

'It's just what?' asked Mack.

'It's just, I can't help thinking that she would have been better off staying at school a little longer. I don't think she's ready to be out in the big, wide, world on her own just yet,' finished Gloop.

'She's done all right on her own before,' said Polly.

'I know,' said Gloop. 'But this is show business. The people are all so shallow. It's all looks, looks, looks.'

Dictionary, who the pencils were all sitting on to get a better view, nodded his head.

'That's exactly right,' said Dictionary. 'You should never judge a book by its cover.'

'Not only that,' continued Gloop, 'I don't want our young, impressionable Penny being told she's too fat, or not pretty enough.'

Polly squinted at the television screen where there was a close-up of Penny looking for clues through a magnifying glass. Penny's body looked ridiculously tiny compared to the size of her magnified eyes.

'She is looking a little thin,' admitted Polly. 'I wonder if we can do anything to help?'

'Send her a package of goodies, perhaps?' suggested Mack.

'How?' said Gloop. 'I'm afraid this time she's got to learn to stand on her own foot.'

'Shhh!' whispered Jade. 'I can't hear what's going on!'

Gloop, Mack and Polly turned their attention back to the television. Penny was triumphantly holding the magnifying glass in one hand, and a sheet of paper titled *Evidence* in the other.

All Ralph and Sarah's writing implements clapped and cheered, then hurried back to their original places before Ralph and Sarah came back to finish their homework.

*

Across the other side of town, Bert the class bully was also tuned in to *Officer Cool*. Unlike Ralph and Sarah, who had already gone back to their homework, Bert kept

watching the credits while his homework
lay abandoned on the table. All of Bert's
writing implements were lying about lazily,
apart from a big, round, black one that was
sitting up watching the television, scowling.

The living-room door burst open and
the black writing implement lay back down
on the table quickly. The spotty clapperboy
from Cool TV skidded into the room.

'Did I miss it?' he asked Bert, his eyes glued to the television set.

'I haven't see you yet,' said Bert, whose eyes were darting from left to right as he read the names scrolling across the screen.

'There I am!' exclaimed the clapperboy as the name Ramsey O'Leary rolled by.

'That's so cool that you have a job on

television, working for *Officer Cool*!' said Bert, very impressed with his older brother.

The black writing implement on the table pricked up its ears at the mention of *Officer Cool*.

'And you, too, can get a great job on TV if you study as hard as I did at school,' said Ramsey the clapperboy, snickering. 'Now go get me a drink and finish your homework.'

'I don't have to get you a drink. Get your own drink!' said Bert angrily.

'I'll tell Mum you were watching TV instead of doing your homework,' Ramsey threatened.

'She won't care, if you're in the show,' said Bert. 'Will she?' he added, a little timidly.

Ramsey gave Bert a look that made Bert realise he'd better do what Ramsey said or else!

In his hurry to get to the kitchen to pour Ramsey a drink, Bert bumped into the table with his homework on it. The big, round, black writing implement rolled off the table and landed on the floor with a loud clatter.

'Clumsy dufus,' said Ramsey, getting off the sofa to look at what had fallen.

Lying on the ground was just the thing

Ramsey needed to write on the front of the clapperboard at Cool TV: a thick, black texta.

'I'll have that,' said Ramsey, shoving the black texta into the back pocket of his black cords, just as Bert came back into the room carrying his drink.

'Thanks,' said Ramsey, taking the drink from Bert. 'And … thanks,' he said again, turning around.

'Hey, how come? What are you thanking me twice for?' Bert asked suspiciously.

But because Ramsey was wearing black cords, Bert couldn't see the black texta smiling smugly from Ramsey's back pocket. Nor did he see Black Texta's

victory smile turn to an expression of
pure disgust as Ramsey's bottom vibrated,
producing a smell that was only rivalled in
its evilness by Black Texta himself!

Chapter 7

Baking Eels

A few days later, filming on the set of *Officer Cool* was not going well.

Rick, dressed as Officer Cool, was leaning with both hands on a desk in an interrogation room at police headquarters, looking genuinely frustrated. The suspect was sitting on the other side of the table, sneering at Rick.

'Cut, cut, cut, cut, cut!' cried Mr Wolf.

Rick turned to Mr Wolf in exasperation.

'What is it this time, Mr Wolf?' Rick asked.

'O'Shea,' said Mr Wolf. 'Have you even read the script?'

'Now let me see …' said Rick, scratching his chin. 'The script, the script …'

'The script!' spat Mr Wolf, brandishing a thick wad of paper in Rick's face.

'Oh. That script,' said Rick, slapping himself on the forehead. 'Of course I've read the script,' he continued angrily. 'I'm a professional.'

'Could have fooled me,' muttered Mr Wolf. 'Any cases of Alzheimer's or amnesia in your family, O'Shea?' he continued.

'Not that it's any of your business, but no,' said Rick.

'Suffered a blow to the head recently?'

continued Mr Wolf. 'Perhaps a mild con-
cussion?'

'What are you getting at?' said Rick,
feeling ruffled.

Mr Wolf thumbed through the script.

'Episode 308. Scene 12. The interrogation
room. The suspect says 'you ain't got nothin'
on me,' and you say … ?' prompted Mr Wolf.

'I've got enough to send you to Alabama
for a long, long time,' recited Rick.

Mr Wolf looked like he was about to
explode with rage.

'No. You. Don't,' yelled Mr Wolf. 'You
say 'I've got enough to send you to *the
slammer* for a long time.' Let's take it from
the top. Aaaaaaaaaaand … action!'

Ramsey the clapperboy held Clappers up
to the camera and pulled his mouth open
slowly. Clappers was sleeping and didn't
notice until …

'Episode 308. Scene 12. Take 2,' said Ramsey, slamming Clappers' teeth together.

Clappers' eyes flew open and he waved his fists threateningly at the clapperboy.

'I'm sending you my dentist bill,' he warned.

Back on the set, Rick leaned over the desk menacingly.

'We can do this the easy way, or the hard way,' he told the suspect.

'You ain't got nothin' on me,' said the suspect.

'I've got enough to send you to *the slammer* for a long time,' said Rick.

'How about we make a deal?'

suggested the suspect, narrowing her eyes.

'I don't bake eels with scum like you –' began Rick.

'Cut!' cried Mr Wolf.

'What now?' said Rick, rolling his eyes.

'You don't *bake eels* with scum like her? Just exactly who do you *bake eels* with, O'Shea?' said Mr Wolf.

Rick shrugged.

'Personally, I don't bake eels with anyone. I'm just saying what's written in the script,' said Rick.

'It says nothing about *baking eels* in the script,' yelled Mr Wolf. 'The suspect has just asked you to make a deal. What's the obvious response?'

'I don't make deals with scum like you,' said Rick. 'But that's not what it says.'

'Oh, no?' said Mr Wolf, thrusting his copy of the script so close to Rick's face

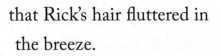

that Rick's hair fluttered in
the breeze.

'Let me see that,' said
Rick, snatching the script
from Mr Wolf.

There, in black-
and-white, it
clearly said, 'I don't
make deals with
scum like you.'

Rick frowned.

'That's not what my copy says,' he said.

Mr Wolf looked at the suspect.

'Hey, suspect. Is that what your copy says?'

The suspect nodded.

Mr Wolf turned to the rest of the crew.

'Any of you got the words *bake eels* in
your copies?'

The crew ruffled through their copies of
the script and shook their heads.

Mr Wolf smiled smugly.

Rick felt stupid.

'Get with the programme, O'Shea,' said Mr Wolf, nastily. 'Everyone, take five. Give O'Shea time to read a copy of the script that didn't come from Narnia.'

As Rick read through the rest of the script, his eyes widened.

'Ahhh,' he said. 'I'm supposed to tell the suspect to put a *sock* in it …'

It took most of the day to finish filming the scene. When work was finally over, Penny lay down on the make-up bench, exhausted. Ruby hopped across and bent over her.

'Penny? Are you okay, honey?' Ruby asked.

Penny was too tired to answer.

'Looks like she had a tough day,' said Wanda. 'We shouldn't have put so much pressure on her –'

A scuffling sound by the door made Ruby and Wanda turn around to see Clappers wriggling in under the door.

'Pressure on her?' said Clappers, dusting himself off. 'If you want pressure, I'll give you pressure. How about two hands, either side of your jaw, slamming your teeth together all day? If O'Shea could just get his lines right …'

At the mention of Rick, Penny stirred.

'It's not Rick's fault –' said Penny weakly.

'Sure it wasn't,' said Clappers sarcastically. 'He didn't make a single mistake all afternoon.'

Clappers turned himself upside-down, flipped his mouth open and sprang up onto the bench to glare at Penny.

'But it wasn't his fault,' protested Penny. 'Someone tampered with his script. You heard him.'

'Yeah. I heard him all right,' said Clappers, doing an Officer Cool impression. "Take cover everyone! He's got a trifle and he's not afraid to goose it."

'Hey!' said Ruby, putting an arm on Clappers to calm him down. 'We're all on the same side here. It's pretty clear to me that someone's been tampering with Rick's script. Maybe we should spend less time fighting and more time trying to find out who it is.'

Penny and Clappers glared at each other a moment longer before turning their attention to Ruby.

'Now Penny …' continued Ruby. 'You've spent all day with Rick. Where did he leave his script?'

Penny thought hard.

'Um … over there on the chair,' she said, pointing to where the script lay on Rick's chair.

'Clappers, would you do us the honour of acquiring the script for us?' Ruby asked sweetly.

Sulkily, Clappers went and fetched the script.

'Now what scene was Rick having trouble with?' said Ruby, thumbing through the script.

'All of them,' mumbled Clappers, as he bent over to read the writing on his front. 'We got as far as scene sixteen.'

'Right,' said Ruby, turning to scene sixteen. She gasped.

'What is it?' asked Penny. She and Clappers hopped over to Ruby and peered over her shoulder to read the script.

Parts of the text had been scribbled out, and new words written over the top in thick, black texta ink. Penny turned white and started to shake.

'Well if pretty boy Rick is too dumb to work out that someone's been tampering with this ...' began Clappers.

'Oh, come on, Clappers,' said Ruby. 'The writers make last minute changes to the script all the time. You know what they're like ...'

'No ...' said Penny softly.

Ruby looked at Penny.

'What?'

'It can't be,' said Penny in a hushed voice.

Ruby and Clappers looked uneasily at each other.

'Can't be what?' asked Clappers.

Penny looked up, her face set.

'I know who did this,' she said.

'You do?' blinked Ruby.

'I'd recognise that ink anywhere,' said Penny.

'You would? Why? Whose is it?' asked Clappers.

'Only the evilest, nastiest, most hateful writing implement ever to set foot in a pencil case,' said Penny.

Ruby and Clappers stared at Penny.

'Well? Who is it?' asked Ruby and Clappers together.

Penny shuddered as she said the name of her old enemy:

'Black Texta.'

'Black who?'

'Black Texta,' repeated Penny. 'He's the most evil villain alive.'

'How do you know him?' asked Clappers.

'We used to live in the same pencil case,' explained Penny. 'Black Texta was horrible. He and his texta army ...'

'Err ... I hate to sound dumb, but what's a teck-stir?' interrupted Wanda.

'Texta,' said Penny. 'You know: marker, felt-tip pen?'

Wanda frowned.

'Like an eye-liner pencil only much, much darker and inkier. And made of plastic,' explained Penny.

'Oh,' said Wanda.

'What about Black Texta's army?' asked Ruby.

'They used to patrol the pencil case and spread rumours about anyone who was getting too popular with our owner, Ralph,' continued Penny. 'In extreme cases they'd give you unnecessary sharpenings and have you expelled!'

'That sounds horrible!' said Clappers. 'As a fellow victim of workplace violence I sympathise completely.'

'So what's Black Texta doing here?' asked Ruby.

'It's obvious, isn't it?' said Clappers, taking Penny's side whole-heartedly. 'He saw Penny on TV and he's come to get her!'

Penny swallowed hard.

'Stop it, Clappers! You're scaring her,' hissed Ruby.

'He might be right,' said Penny. 'We thought we'd got rid of Black Texta for good, but he came back once, so he can come back twice.'

'Tracking you down here seems like a bit of a stretch,' said Ruby.

'Maybe, but I wouldn't put anything past that evil implement,' said Penny.

'So what are we going to do?' asked Wanda.

'Clappers, Ruby, you're coming with me,' said Penny. 'We're going to stop Black Texta meddling with the scripts.'

'What about me?' whined Wanda.

'Uh,' said Penny, noticing Ruby shaking her head firmly, 'you stay here and stay plugged in so you can melt that black plastic fiend if he sets foot inside the trailer.'

'Okay,' said Wanda, clicking her tongs together like she meant business.

'Let's go,' Penny said, and Clappers and Ruby followed her out the trailer door and into the night.

Chapter 8

The lamp-beast

Penny strode through the car park and into the studio building so fast that Clappers and Ruby had trouble keeping up.

'Where are we going?' panted Ruby.

'To find Meg,' said Penny without turning around.

'And how is Meg going to help us?' asked Clappers. 'Are you going to have her scare the wits out of this Black Texta bloke by whispering at him?'

As they got to the corner Penny stopped short. Ruby and Clappers both crashed into her, making Clappers clatter noisily to the ground. Clappers landed flat on his back and, like a stranded turtle, could not get back up.

'Hey. Would one of you lovely ladies mind giving me a hand?' Clappers asked.

Ruby stretched a hand out towards Clappers when suddenly there was the sound of heavy footsteps. Penny grabbed Ruby's other hand and yanked her into a doorway, out of sight.

'Hey!' yelled Clappers. 'Don't leave me here. It sounds like it's getting closer …'

Two shiny, black shoes appeared around the corner. Clappers lay stock-still, trying to blend into the floor.

But it was no good. A hand, belonging
to the security guard who was wearing
the shiny black shoes, reached down and
picked up Clappers.

'Now where did you come from?' said
the security guard, reading the writing
on Clappers' front. '*Officer Cool*, eh? We'd
better put you back in Studio Three.'

When the guard and Clappers had

moved a safe distance away, Penny and Ruby came out of their hidey hole and followed behind them stealthily.

Penny and Ruby paused in the shadows while the security guard unlocked the door to Studio Three. As the guard's feet disappeared through the doorway, Penny and Ruby hopped swiftly to follow him in before the door closed.

The security guard dumped Clappers on the director's chair and turned to leave. Once the door had closed safely behind him, Penny and Ruby hopped towards the director's chair and used the criss-cross chair legs as a climbing frame to somersault up onto the seat of the chair.

When they got to the top, Clappers was angry.

'Thanks for leaving me there,' he said.

'Sorry, Clappers, but we couldn't have

helped you and avoided being seen at the same time,' explained Penny. 'You have to agree – it would have looked a bit suspicious: a clapperboard, a pencil and a make-up brush all lying on the floor together. The guard might have taken us to the watch tower, instead of Studio Three. And we don't have a moment to lose!'

'My goodness Penny, you've got a good head on your neck,' said Ruby.

At that moment, something landed on the arm-rest of Mr Wolf's chair, almost making it topple over. It was Meg.

'What's going on?' she asked.

'Someone's been fiddling with Rick's scripts,' said Clappers.

'What do you mean by fiddling?' asked Meg.

'Crossing out the words and writing new, stupid ones,' explained Penny.

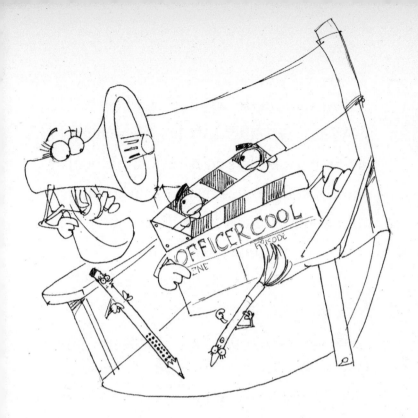

'Are you sure?' Meg asked.

'Yes,' said Ruby. 'Rick left his script in the dressing-room. We were looking at it just now. It's got scribbling out and new writing all over it.'

'Well that's not too unusual –' said Meg.

'But that's not all. Tell her the rest, Penny,' said Clappers.

'I recognised the writing,' said Penny.

'Whose was it? Mr Wolf's? He's always had it in for Rick,' said Meg. 'Or maybe that new co-star. Most of the guests who come on the show secretly want Rick's job –'

'It's not a human,' said Penny.

'It's not? You mean … one of us?' said Meg in shock.

'No. Nobody working on the show,' said Penny. 'When I told Ruby and Clappers they'd never heard of him.'

'Heard of who?' asked Meg.

'Black Texta,' said Penny.

Penny quickly explained to Meg all about Black Texta.

'This Black Texta sounds like a nasty piece of work,' said Meg.

'Oh, he's a nasty piece of work, all right,' said Penny.

'Are you sure it's him?' asked Meg.

'Yes,' said Penny. 'I'd recognise that writing anywhere.'

'With the pressure from the network about canning the show, this couldn't have come at a worse time,' said Meg.

'It's always a "worse time" when Black Texta is around,' said Penny darkly. 'Believe me, with Black Texta on the loose, the possibility that the network might can the show is the least of our worries.'

'Maybe we should just forget about fixing the script and start looking for Black Texta instead,' suggested Clappers.

Penny thought for a moment.

'No. Knowing Black Texta, it'll be a while before he shows himself,' said Penny. 'He's getting more and more cunning with more complex plans. But we should be careful. The script tampering could be a trap.'

Ruby, Clappers and Meg nodded, looking serious.

'Meg, where does Mr Wolf keep the master copy of the script?' asked Penny.

'He always has it with him during filming,' said Meg. 'But at night he keeps it in his office. Under lock and key.'

'Can we get in there?' asked Penny.

'I think so,' said Meg.

'Let's go,' said Penny. 'And keep your eyes peeled for Black Texta!'

Penny, Meg, Ruby and Clappers marched to the door of the studio. Penny checked that the coast was clear, then beckoned to the others to join her in the corridor.

'Okay, Meg. Lead the way to Mr Wolf's office,' said Penny.

The strange band of friends followed Meg along the corridor towards the studio executives' suites. Ruby, Clappers and

Penny had never been in that part of the
building before. It was much nicer than
the rest of Cool TV studios, with carpet
and potted plants and even a chocolate
vending machine.

'Are we there yet?' asked Clappers.

'Hmmm. It shouldn't be much further
now,' said Meg, reading out the names on
the doors. 'Hughes … A.Fraid … Ovdabig
… Badd … Wolf. Here it is.'

They stood in front of Mr Wolf's door.

'Clappers, help me up to the handle and

I'll open the door,' said Penny.

Penny climbed on top of Clappers and Clappers hurled his mouth open, flinging Penny up to the door handle.

Penny jumped up and down on the handle, but it wouldn't budge.

'It's locked,' she said.

'Right then, Clappers, you slide under, and get the script,' said Ruby.

Meg shook her head.

'The script's too fat. It'll never fit under the door,' said Meg.

'That's okay,' Penny called from her spot on the door handle, peering through the keyhole. 'I can see the keys. They're on the desk.'

'Okay then, Clappers,'

said Ruby. 'Get the keys, unlock the door, and then get the script.'

'Right,' said Clappers, wriggling under the door.

'Oh! Watch out for the ...' began Meg, but Clappers had already disappeared.

'Watch out for the what?' said Penny, peering through the keyhole.

'The lamp,' said Meg.

'What's wrong with the lamp?' asked Penny as she watched Clappers slide out the other side of the door and head straight towards Mr Wolf's desk.

The desk was completely bare except for the master script and a 'CUJO' brand desk lamp which was casting eerie shadows around the room. Directly under the lamp on the top of the desk was a small circle of light with something bright glinting in the centre of it: the keys.

'The keys are right under the lamp,' squeaked Penny, turning to the others in panic.

'Oh, dear,' said Meg, shaking her head.

By the time Penny had poked her head back through the keyhole, Clappers was on the desk. But the keys were nowhere to be seen.

Scratching his head, Clappers walked right into the middle of the circle of light, directly under the lamp.

'That's weird. They were there a moment ago ...' said Penny.

A low growl made Clappers look around. He expected to see Black Texta towering over him, but there was nothing around apart from the lamp and the master script. Clappers continued looking for the keys until a second, louder growl made him stop short. Trembling a little, he looked at the lamp directly above him.

The lamp had sprouted teeth and looked like a very mean guard dog. It bent low over Clappers and barked.

Clappers turned and ran. The lamp-beast chased after him, snapping at his heels, before being pulled up short by its cord.

'What's happening in there?' asked Ruby,

who could hear the barking out in the corridor.

'The lamp's after him,' said Penny.

'I told him to watch out for the lamp,' said Meg.

With his back hard up against the office wall, Clappers tried to tip-toe around the snarling lamp-beast. The cord kept it at bay, but Clappers couldn't get to the desk. The beast had blocked him off.

As Clappers shuffled around the wall of the office, Penny noticed the lamp-beast's cord was winding around the base of Mr Wolf's chair and getting a little shorter.

'Clappers,' called Penny through the key hole. 'Walk in circles around the chair.'

'What?' said Clappers. 'Are you crazy? Can't you see the size of its teeth?'

'Are you trying to get Clappers killed?' asked Meg.

'Trust me, Clappers,' said Penny. 'Go around the chair in the one direction. But keep your distance.'

'Okay …' said Clappers doubtfully.

Clappers gingerly took a couple of steps to the right. The lamp beast followed him, but was pulled a little further back by its cord with every step. Clappers got to the wall and poked his toe around the corner. The lamp-beast jumped at him but the cord held him back safely. As Clappers inched his way around the room, the lamp-beast's cord wound around the chair getting shorter and shorter until the beast was pulled up short, unable to move.

'Okay now, Clappers,' said Penny. 'It should be safe to get the script.'

Clappers seized his chance to clamber onto the desk and grab the keys and the master copy of the script. He didn't notice the plug at the end of the lamp-beast's cord slowly coming out of the wall socket.

As Clappers struggled with the heavy script, the plug at the end of the lamp-beast's cord came even further out of the socket. When Clappers finally made it to the door he threw the keys up to Penny. Penny unlocked the door and tossed the keys back towards Mr Wolf's desk.

Just like a dog chasing after a ball, the lamp-beast leaped up to catch the keys in its mouth. With the extra tug, the plug at the end of the lamp-beast's cord came free of the socket.

Penny, Clappers and the lamp-beast itself saw the cord fly off the edge of the desk and realised the lamp-beast was free.

'Run, Clappers!' called Penny.

Clappers picked up the master script and hurried through the door as the lamp-beast lunged at him.

'Clappers! The door!' called Penny, but it was too late. Clappers was already half-way down the hall, and the lamp-beast had its head through the door, snarling at Meg and Ruby.

'What do we do?' cried Meg, who was holding the door shut as best she could.

'We run like the Clappers!' said Penny, leaping off the door handle.

Penny, Meg and Ruby sprinted down the hallway, the lamp-beast close behind.

'Are we going the right way?' asked Penny.

'I don't know!' said Meg.

They clattered past a bathroom just as the security guard with the shiny black shoes was coming out of it.

'Hey, what the … ?' said the security guard, doing a double-take as he saw what looked like a pencil, a megaphone and a make-up brush running down the corridor.

As the lamp-beast passed, the security guard stuck out a shiny, black foot and stepped on its cord. The lamp-beast stopped short.

The security guard picked up the lamp
and took it back to Mr Wolf's office,
shaking his head saying, 'My wife's right.
I really have been doing these night shifts
too long.'

When Meg, Ruby and Penny were safely
back in Rick's trailer Ruby rounded on
Clappers.

'Thanks for leaving us there,' she said.

'Sorry, but I couldn't have helped you

and avoided being bitten at the same time,' said Clappers.

Meg took the script and leafed through it.

'Black Texta has scribbled out just about everything on the last few pages.'

'Just as I suspected,' said Penny. 'Black Texta's moved on from wrecking just Rick's script, to wrecking the master script. When Mr Wolf's secretary copies the scripts tomorrow morning, they'll all be the same, but they'll all be wrong.'

'That will ruin the whole show!' said Ruby.

'And we'll all be out of a job,' wailed Meg. 'What are we going to do?'

'Get me some blank paper,' said Penny.

'How's that going to help?' asked Clappers.

'You'll see,' said Penny. 'Just get me the paper.'

Chapter 9

Back in the beast's lair

Penny worked all night to fix the pages of
the master script Black Texta had ruined.
It took her until well after the sun was up
until she was happy with the story.

'Ralph should like that,' thought Penny
to herself, yawning and closing the heavy
cover of the script book.

She looked around, and saw that Clappers, Meg and all the beauty applicators were fast asleep. Penny tried to drag the script with her to the doorway of Rick's trailer, but it was too heavy. Although she didn't want to wake the others, Penny knew she would need help. She hopped over to Clappers.

'Clappers. Clappers. Wake up!' Penny hissed in Clappers' ear.

But Clappers didn't stir.

Penny put a hand on Clappers' shoulder and shook him gently.

'No, no! Get away from me you evil pooch!' said Clappers, pulling away from Penny in fright before waking up properly.

'Clappers. It's me, Penny. It was only a dream,' said Penny soothingly.

Clappers' eyes darted around the room quickly, before resting on Penny.

'Phew!' said Clappers. 'I thought …
never mind. Looks like the sun's up. I'd
better get back to the studio,' he continued,
getting to his feet.

'On your way
back, could you
drop this off in Mr
Wolf's office?' said
Penny, presenting
Clappers with the
master script and
her most winning
smile.

'Sure,' yawned
Clappers. 'I'll drop it off in Wolf's office
- Wolf's office?! Are you crazy?!' he yelled,
coming to his senses. 'I almost got killed in
there last night!'

'I can't manage it all on my own, it's too
heavy,' said Penny.

'Fine,' said Clappers. 'But I'm not going in there alone.'

'Don't worry,' said Penny, smiling. 'You won't need to go in there at all.'

Penny and Clappers crept along the air-conditioning duct towards Mr Wolf's office.

'Why didn't you think of this last night?' asked Clappers as he kicked the script ahead of them along the duct.

'I didn't get the idea until I read about Officer Cool chasing a baddie through an air-conditioning duct in the script,' said Penny. 'And I couldn't have read the script unless you'd already gone in there and got it, could I?'

'We could have got a fishing rod or something from the props department,' Clappers grumbled.

'Then that's what we'll do tonight,' said Penny, stopping short. 'We're here.'

Penny peered through the grill of the air-conditioning vent down into Mr Wolf's office. The lamp-beast was sleeping peacefully under the chair, facing the door with its body curled tightly around the keys.

'Aw, look at him asleep,' said Clappers. 'Don't you just want to go and pat him?'

'Are you completely insane?' said Penny.

'It was a joke,' said Clappers, yanking on the grill. 'The hairs on the back of my neck are standing on end just looking at him.'

Clappers dropped the grill on the floor of the air-conditioning duct with a loud clatter.

The lamp-beast woke up and looked around.

'Uh-ho,' said Penny.

'What's the problem? There's no way he can get to us up here,' said Clappers, kicking the script out of the duct so that it landed on the desk with a dull thud.

'It's upside-down,' said Penny.

'What?' said Clappers, heaving the grill up to put it back in place.

'The script's upside-down,' said Penny. 'Mr Wolf might notice. We have to get in there and flip it.'

'Are you kidding?' said Clappers, dropping the grill and peering over the edge of the vent.

As he did so, the lamp-beast leaped at the vent.

'Aargh!' cried Clappers, backing away from the snarling lamp-beast.

'The grill! The grill!' said Penny, trying to lift the grill and pass it to Clappers.

'The grill? What about that upside-down

script you were so worried about?' asked Clappers.

'That was before I saw its teeth up close,' said Penny, struggling with the grill.

Penny and Clappers pushed with all their might and managed to get the grill into place, sealing the lamp-beast outside and the two of them safely inside.

'Let's get out of here before it works out how to chew through steel,' said Penny.

Clappers didn't need telling twice, and the two of them bounded along the air-conditioning duct and back to the safety of Rick's trailer.

Chapter 10

A show-saving plan

During filming later that day, Penny was silently mouthing the lines she had made up as the actors spoke them.

'And that's how I knew it was a forgery. Being a policeman helps you know "write" from wrong,' said Rick, in his Officer Cool character.

'Aaaaaaaaaaaand … cut!' said Mr Wolf.

'Thank you people. That's a wrap.'

The cast and crew all clapped each other and headed for the door. They all stopped, however, when a man in a pin-striped suit appeared from the shadows at the back of the studio and clapped a hand on Mr Wolf's shoulder.

'Great work, Lyall,' said the man in the pin-striped suit.

'Why thank you, Mr Goldman,' said Mr Wolf. 'It's an honour to have you on the set, sir.'

'I only saw the last few scenes,' continued Mr Goldman. 'That was great writing. Did you hire someone new?'

Before Mr Wolf could answer, the studio door burst open and a badly-dressed man with unkempt hair and a pencil behind his ear stormed in, brandishing a script.

'Mr Wolf!' shouted the badly-dressed

man. 'What do you mean by this? This is not the script I wrote. Have you got someone in behind my back? Because I have a contract and I'm gonna –'

Mr Wolf put an arm around the badly-dressed writer and tried to calm him down.

'Marty, Marty. You crack me up with your sense of humour,' said Mr Wolf, forcing a laugh. 'I haven't got anyone new in, and that script's been locked in my office the whole time. Mr Goldman, the studio executive, was just saying how great the writing was.'

Marty stopped glaring at Mr Wolf and looked at Mr Goldman. He adjusted his collar and calmed down immediately.

'Why thank you, Mr Goldman,' said

Marty modestly. 'I'm pleased you enjoyed my work. I'd better get back to working on the next episode.'

'Unfortunately that won't be necessary,' said Mr Goldman.

The entire cast and crew went deathly quiet as everyone hung on Mr Goldman's next words.

'I hate to break it to you this way,' continued Mr Goldman, 'but I just came back from the studio meeting. They've decided to cancel *Officer Cool*.'

Penny peered out of Rick's pocket.

'I ... I don't understand,' said Mr Wolf. 'You just said you really liked the last few scenes –'

'And I believe you used the phrase "great writing" ...' said Marty.

The rest of the cast muttered amongst themselves until Mr Goldman held up his hand for silence.

'You know I love the show,' said Mr Goldman. 'And the work you all did this afternoon is even better than your normal high standard. Unfortunately we're just not getting the ratings.'

'Ratings, schmatings!' said Mr Wolf, angrily. 'You know those numbers don't mean anything.'

'How so, Lyall?' asked Mr Goldman, who knew the network lived and breathed on ratings numbers.

'People never tell the truth,' said Mr Wolf. 'How many housewives admit to watching *Days of Our Lives*?'

'It's a really good show,' muttered Shanna.

'And how many men say they're staying home to mow the lawn, when the real reason they won't go shopping with their wives is because they want to watch the Saturday afternoon football match?' asked Mr Wolf, warming to his subject.

All the men laughed sheepishly.

'And how many children,' said Mr Wolf, looking very pleased with himself indeed, 'admit to watching afternoon television when their parents think they're doing their homework?'

Mr Goldman raised an eyebrow.

'Good point, Lyall,' he said. 'Look, I tell you what. If you can think of a way to prove that lots of kids watch *Officer Cool* by the end of the week, I can save the show. Otherwise …' Mr Goldman drew a finger across his throat sharply. And with that he left the studio.

Mr Wolf turned to the cast and crew.

'Okay people, you heard the man. If you

want to keep your jobs, I need an idea from each of you on my chair tomorrow before shooting.'

*

Back in Rick's dressing-room, the beauty applicators, Clappers and Meg all gathered around Penny as she explained the situation to them.

'... so we have to think of something by tomorrow,' said Penny.

'That doesn't give us much time,' said Meg.

'We have to think hard,' said Ruby.

'But I'm not used to thinking. I'm more a looks kind of girl than a brainiac,' said Wanda.

'That's okay,' said Penny. 'I've already come up with something. Tell me what you think of this ...'

The creatures all bent their heads in

towards Penny as she whispered her plan to them.

*

In Studio Three the next day, the cast and crew were gathered around Mr Wolf as he plucked sheets of paper from his chair, unfolded them and read them aloud.

'We could have characters from *Days of Our Lives* make guest appearances.'

Mr Wolf screwed up the piece of paper.

'Nice try Shanna, but different network.'
Shanna blushed.

Mr Wolf tossed the ball of paper over his shoulder, where it joined a growing pile of scrunched-up paper on the ground before picking up the next suggestion.

'We could make the show educational by adding an *Officer Cool safety tip of the day* at the end. Do you people really think kids want more education? They get enough of that at school,' said Mr Wolf, balling up the piece of paper.

'But –' began Rick.

Mr Wolf glared at Rick as he tossed the ball of paper over his shoulder. Thinking that it was hopeless and the show was doomed, Mr Wolf picked up the last piece of paper and read it silently. His expression softened, and by the time he got to the end he was actually smiling.

He turned the piece of paper over, then looked back at the cast and crew.

'There's no name on this suggestion, but I think it might be the answer!' said Mr Wolf excitedly. 'We could have a competition where children write in to appear as a *special guest star* on *Officer Cool*. The number of entries will prove how popular *Officer Cool* is.'

Mr Wolf looked up. The cast and crew all nodded and chattered excitedly about the suggestion.

Penny, who was sitting in her usual spot in Rick's pocket, smiled proudly.

'This is it, people,' said Mr Wolf, waving the piece of paper above his head triumphantly. 'We'll show them once and for all just how cool *Officer Cool* really is. Now places everybody. Aaaaaaaaaaand … action!'

Ramsey the clapperboy brought

Clappers up in front of the camera. This time Clappers was wide awake, and frightened.

'Episode 311. Scene 1. Take 1,' said Ramsey.

'Look,' said Clappers, trying to bargain. 'You don't have to do this. We can come to an arrangement … you don't have to do this …!'

Ramsey prised Clappers' jaws apart.

'You don't have to do this …' said Clappers, as best he could with his mouth wide open.

But Ramsey couldn't hear him, and slammed Clappers' teeth together harder than ever.

Clappers reverberated with the impact.

'You had to do that, didn't you?' said the wobbling Clappers.

Chapter 11

Bert's triumph

As usual Ralph and Sarah were just getting up to turn off the television and finish their homework when there was a pause in the *Officer Cool* theme music and *Officer Cool* appeared on the screen.

'Hey kids. Have you ever wanted to be on television?' said Officer Cool. 'Cool TV is giving you the chance to co-star, with me, on an episode of *Officer Cool*. All you have to do is write in twenty-five words or less why you're *Officer Cool's* biggest fan.'

Officer Cool's smiling face froze, and a second voice that sounded nothing at all like Officer Cool said, in double-quick time, 'Entries must be received no later than 5 p.m. on Friday the 13th. Judges' decision is final and no correspondence will be entered into. All entries remain the property of Cool TV. Cast and crew at Cool TV and their immediate families are ineligible to enter.'

'Wow! Did you see that?' said Sarah.

'How Officer Cool could say all those things without moving his lips?' asked Ralph.

'No. The competition to co-star on *Officer*

Cool,' said Sarah. 'I'm going to enter.'

'Me too,' said Ralph.

'I'm going to win,' said Sarah.

'Me too,' said Ralph.

'Don't be silly, Ralph. We can't both win,' said Sarah.

'Well you'd better get used to knowing what it feels like to be a loser,' said Ralph.

'I'm not a loser. You're the loser,' said Sarah.

'Who's the bigger loser: Loser or Friend of Loser?' challenged Ralph.

Sarah thought for a moment, then realised she had no idea how to answer Ralph's question. Instead, she grabbed a pencil and paper and started writing furiously.

Ralph leaned over to see what Sarah was writing, but she hunched her shoulder over the paper and moved away. When she had finished writing, Sarah counted the words.

'Twenty-seven,' she said in disgust, screwing up her paper and starting again.

Ralph was having an equally hard time coming up with a twenty-five-word answer to explain why he was *Officer Cool*'s biggest fan.

After several false starts each, Ralph and Sarah were finally happy with their entries.

'Finished writing the losing entry?' asked Ralph, passing Sarah an envelope.

'I think you're mistaken. This is the winning entry,' said Sarah.

'We'll let Officer Cool decide,' said Ralph.

*

When the Friday mail arrived at Cool TV, Mr Wolf had the pleasure of emptying an entire sack full of entries from *Officer Cool* fans onto Mr Goldman's desk.

'Nine thousand nine hundred and ninety-eight, nine thousand nine hundred and ninety-nine, ten thousand!' said Mr Wolf proudly, counting out the envelopes.

'Okay, okay. I get your point,' said Mr Goldman, smiling broadly. 'A lot of kids are watching *Officer Cool*. I'll take these numbers to the board meeting on Monday. There's no way they can cancel the show with proof like this. Good work, Lyall!'

Mr Wolf smiled.

'Although, you do realise the problem

you've got now, don't you?' said Mr
Goldman, suddenly serious.

'Problem?' said Mr Wolf.

'Yeah. You've got to read through all
these and pick a winner,' said Mr Goldman
smiling again. 'Enjoy your weekend!'

And with that Mr Goldman left the office.

Mr Wolf stared after him then looked at
the mound of entries. He shook his head
and began reading.

Penny, who had overheard Mr Wolf and
Mr Goldman talking on her way to Mr
Wolf's office via the air-conditioning duct,
smiled and hurried back to Rick's trailer

to tell everyone the good
news. In her excitement,
she didn't notice a dark
figure following her.

Meg, Clappers and all
the beauty applicators

mobbed Penny the moment she squeezed in under the door.

'So? How'd it go?' asked Meg eagerly.

'It worked!' said Penny. 'They got ten thousand entries! Mr Wolf is in Mr Goldberg's office right now, trying to choose the winner. And Mr Goldberg said he's not allowed to go home until he's chosen the best one!'

'Well done, Penny,' said Ruby. 'You've saved the show.'

Penny blushed.

'Well, it wasn't just me. Think of all the other pencils out there who helped the fans write all those entries …'

'Come, come, now Penny. You did brilliantly,' said Clappers. 'Let's have three cheers for Penny. Hip hip …'

'Hooray!' cried all the beauty applicators.

Outside Rick's dressing-room, the dark

figure who had followed Penny along the
air-conditioning duct and back to Rick's
trailer was listening at the door.

'Hmmmmmph,' said Black Texta,
sneering and turning away from the door
just in time to see a hand close its fingers
around him and lift him up into the air.

For the first time in a long time, Black
Texta actually felt frightened.

'There you are. I'd been wondering where

you'd got to,' said the owner of the hand,
Ramsey the clapperboy.

'What? Oh no ...' said Black Texta.

Ramsey shoved Black Texta into his
jeans pocket and sauntered towards his
car. Remembering his last experience
in Ramsey's back pocket, Black Texta
pulled his cap down tightly over his
nose. But it wasn't enough to mask the
accompanying foul smell of Ramsey's
bottom vibrations.

Ramsey got to his car and started
fumbling in all his pockets for his keys.

'Rats,' said Ramsey. 'I must have left my
keys in the studio.'

Ramsey walked back across the car
park and into the studio building. As he
walked past Mr Goldman's office, Mr
Wolf looked up.

'Hey, um, you!' called Mr Wolf, unable to

remember the clapperboy's name.

Ramsey poked his head around the doorway.

'Off home now?' asked Mr Wolf.

'Just came back to pick up my keys,' said Ramsey.

'How'd you like to earn a quick hundred bucks?' said Mr Wolf, smiling like a used car salesman.

*

The following Monday Ralph and Sarah
ran all the way home from school.

'I can't believe today's the day they're
going to make the big announcement,' said
Ralph.

'I've waited the whole weekend for this,'
said Sarah, trailing behind.

'Come on,' said Ralph, holding the
gate open. 'We don't want to miss hearing
Officer Cool call my name out.'

'I didn't know your name was Sarah
Monaghan,' puffed Sarah, resting on the
gatepost.

Ralph was already on the porch, holding
the front door open for Sarah.

'Come on,' said Ralph. 'It starts in two
minutes!'

The children ran inside, letting the
screen door slam behind them. Ralph
dropped his school bag and turned on the

television just in time to see a police car drive up with *Officer Cool* at the wheel.

Ralph and Sarah's writing implements peaked out of the children's schoolbags to watch too.

On the television, Officer Cool was rolling down the window.

'Hi, kids,' said Officer Cool. 'All of us here on *Officer Cool* at Cool TV want to thank you for writing in to our competition. We received thousands of entries, and they were all of a really high standard.'

Sarah and Ralph smiled at each other.

'See?' said Sarah. 'You came a close second.'

'Unfortunately there can be only one winner ...' continued Officer Cool.

'Yeah, me,' said Ralph.

'And the winner is ...'

Penny peered over the rim of Officer Cool's pocket as he opened the envelope.

Sarah and Ralph crossed their fingers.

'… Bert O'Leary!'

Penny was horrified.

So were Sarah and Ralph.

'Bert?' said Ralph

'Bert the *bully*?' said Sarah

They gaped at each other in disbelief.

*

The next day at school, Ralph and Sarah had to fight to get to their desk. Due to winning the competition, Bert had become the most popular boy in school. The whole class was gathered around Bert, asking him questions and telling him how great they thought he was.

'I can't believe he won,' said Ralph through gritted teeth.

'I can't believe I lost,' said Sarah, shaking her head in disbelief.

'Were you surprised you won, Bert?' asked Malcolm.

'No,' boasted Bert, trying to sound bored as though winning competitions and appearing on television happened to him every day. 'I kind of expected it.'

'When's your show going to be on TV, Bert?' asked Lucy Williams.

'It's supposed to be a secret, but I guess I can tell you. The 11th of August,' said Bert.

'Remind me to book a dentist appointment for that afternoon,' Ralph muttered to Sarah.

Bert leaned forward and sneered at Ralph.

'You won't get out of seeing me that easily, Ralphie,' said Bert nastily, before turning his attention back to his fan club.

'What was that supposed to mean?' Ralph asked Sarah.

'I don't know,' said Sarah. 'Maybe he's planning to bring in a video for show and tell.'

'That's a great idea,' interrupted Bert. 'You're not just an ugly face, Monaghan.'

Chapter 12

Facing the enemy

Although Penny was disappointed that
neither Ralph nor Sarah had won the
Officer Cool competition, she tried not to
show it as the beauty applicators all talked
about the special episode. Excitement
had reached an all-time high two days

before filming of the special episode, when suddenly Rick's trailer door burst open. Meg stood in the doorway, panting.

'Look what happened to Clappers,' she whispered breathlessly.

'What?' said Ruby.

'I said,' said Meg, turning up her volume control to maximum, 'LOOK WHAT HAPPENED TO CLAPPERS!'

Penny and the beauty applicators gathered together on the edge of the bench.

'It's okay, Clappers. They can help you,' coaxed Meg gently.

Slowly, Clappers took a step forward to stand in the middle of the doorway. He had streaks of black ink all over him and hung his head in shame.

The beauty applicators all bounded off the bench to get a closer look, but Penny stayed where she was, shaking. Even from such a long distance away, she recognised the black ink instantly.

'Clappers. What happened?' said Ruby, trying to rub the black texta ink off Clappers' front, with no success.

Clappers looked across sadly at Penny.

'I met your friend, that Black Texta dude,' said Clappers weakly. 'He is one nasty piece of work.'

'When did he do this to you?' asked Penny.

'Just after filming,' said Clappers. 'He was in the back pocket of that horrid clapperboy who keeps ramming my teeth together. He slipped out of the pocket when the twerp bent over to switch off the camera. I didn't think anything of it at first, but as soon as the last human left the studio he came at me.'

'Where is he now?' asked Penny.

'I don't know,' said Clappers. 'It all happened so fast ...' Clappers trailed off and started weeping.

'That's okay, Clappers,' said Penny. 'It's all my fault. I should never have come here. The show almost gets cancelled because of me, and now Black Texta's attacking my friends ... It's probably best if I just go.'

'If that's what you really want ...' said Ruby.

Penny hopped towards the door.

'What are you doing?' said Meg, standing in her way.

'I'm … I'm leaving …' said Penny. 'I've caused nothing but trouble since I got here.'

'That's not true,' said Meg. 'The show was in trouble long before you came on board, Penny. And if you hadn't come up with the brilliant idea of having a competition to prove how many children love *Officer Cool*, we'd all be out of a job.'

All the beauty applicators nodded.

'And think of all the children out there,' added Wanda. 'They wouldn't be able to watch *Officer Cool* if it wasn't for you.'

'Yeah, Penny,' said Clappers. 'I think this Black Texta fella would have made his mark even if you hadn't come on the show.'

'Besides, you can't go before you've helped us deal with Black Texta,' said Meg firmly. 'You've beaten him before, and we can't do it without you. Not all of us are tough enough to look after ourselves like Clappers.'

'Ouch!' said Clappers as Ruby accidentally poked him in the eye with a cotton ball.

'See?' said Meg. 'We need you.'

Penny looked around at Clappers, Meg and the beauty applicators. Meg was right. They needed her help to defeat Black Texta.

'Okay. I'll stay,' said Penny. 'But we're

going to have to be extra careful from now on. Nobody is to go anywhere by themselves.'

'Got it, always travel in pairs,' said Meg.

'What else?' asked Ruby.

'Getting rid of Black Texta, once and for all,' said Penny.

'How are we going to do that?' asked Clappers.

Penny thought for a moment, and then the answer was so obvious she was surprised she hadn't thought of it before.

'With help from our friend Cujo,' she said, smiling.

'Who's Cujo … you don't mean the lamp-beast?' said Ruby.

'Look, I don't know if you've forgotten already, but that thing tried to kill us.

Twice!' began Clappers.

'How are you even going to talk to it?' asked Meg.

'I'm not,' said Penny, rolling her eyes. 'We just lure Black Texta into Mr Wolf's office, and Cujo will do the rest.'

'Ah!' said Meg, nodding sagely.

'How do we lure Black Texta into Mr Wolf's office?' asked Ruby.

'Easy,' said Penny, smiling knowingly. 'Now you guys just keep Black Texta away from the script during filming tomorrow, and I'll do the rest.'

*

Penny may have made it sound easy, but Clappers was having a hard time keeping up his part of the plan. Mr Wolf had taken Meg with him when the *Officer Cool* cast and crew were on their lunch break, and

Clappers was left guarding the master
script all on his own.

'Just keep Black Texta away from the
master script, indeed!' Clappers muttered
to himself as he stood bravely between the
master script and Black Texta, dodging
blow after inky blow.

'You can't fend me off forever, Clicky,'
said Black Texta menacingly, lunging at
Clappers again.

'But I can,' said a small voice behind them.

Black Texta turned around slowly.

'Ms Penny Pencil,' sneered Black Texta.

'I was wondering when we'd meet again.'

'Always too soon for my liking,' said Penny, trying not to shudder as she faced her old enemy.

'Nice outfit,' said Black Texta, eyeing Penny's police costume. 'But do you really think it's going to protect you?'

'Oh, I know it's what's on the inside that counts,' said Penny.

Black Texta took a step towards Penny. Penny did her best not to flinch.

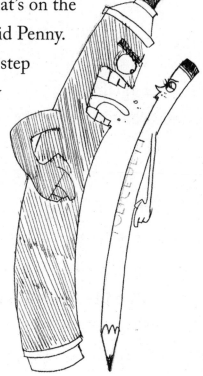

'We're quite brave nowadays, aren't we?' said Black Texta.

'I'm not afraid of you,' said Penny.

'Well you should be!' bellowed Black

Texta, making Clappers, at least, feel very frightened indeed.

'Should I?' said Penny, trying to keep her voice even. 'Your little script changing plan hasn't been working very well, has it?'

Black Texta's eyes narrowed.

'I thought you might have had something to do with that,' said Black Texta.

'Yes,' said Penny. 'You cross out the bad bits, and I write better bits. Quite a nice team effort, actually.'

'Not exactly as I'd planned,' said Black Texta. 'I'd be curious to know how you got hold of the script,' he continued conversationally.

Penny ignored his last remark.

'It's getting quite annoying, having that writer fellow taking all the credit for my work, rewriting all the pages you've wrecked,' said Penny, choosing her words carefully. 'But I'd imagine it's even more frustrating for you, Black Texta, the scripts actually being *better* after you've dabbled with them, instead of worse.'

'Hmmm,' said Black Texta.

'You have to admit,' said Penny, 'it'd be better for everyone if you just stopped tampering, wouldn't it?'

Black Texta glared at Penny.

'I mean, your plan's backfiring, your ink must be running pretty low … Face it. You've lost this time, Black Texta,' said Penny.

Penny watched Black Texta carefully. His shoulders slumped, but there was still an evil glint in his eye, just as Penny had suspected there would be.

'You're right. You've outdone me this time, Penny Pencil,' said Black Texta. 'But tell me: how did you do it?'

'It was quite simple really,' began Penny.

'Just a matter of breaking into Mr Wolf's office and altering the script …'

'Penny, no!' said Clappers. 'Don't tell him anything.'

'It doesn't matter, Clappers,' said Penny. 'Look at him. He's in hardly any state to go into Mr Wolf's office …'

Penny trailed off at the sound of approaching footsteps. By the time the first human opened the door to Studio Three, Penny, Clappers and Black Texta were lying exactly where Rick and the clapperboy had left them before going to lunch.

*

That night when Clappers wriggled under the door into Rick's trailer, Penny was waiting for him eagerly.

'That was some performance, Penny!' said Clappers.

'Do you think he fell for it?' asked Penny.

'Hook, line and Inker! Black Texta was so lost in devious thoughts all afternoon, he didn't even bother attacking me,' said Clappers. 'I reckon he'll be breaking into Wolf's office at the first opportunity.'

'And Cujo will be waiting for him,' said Penny smiling.

Chapter 13

The special guest star

The day of Bert's big shoot was unbearable for Ralph and Sarah. Bert was strutting around school like he used to in the height of his bullying days. When the bell finally rang, Bert was first out of the classroom, surrounded by a gaggle of fans. Ralph and Sarah waited until Bert and his cronies were all gone before leaving the classroom themselves.

As they walked down the steps at the front of the school a car horn tooted. Ralph looked up and saw his mother waving at them from the car.

'That's Mum. What's she doing? She never picks us up from school,' said Ralph.

'Quick, quick, put your schoolbags in the boot. I have a surprise for you,' called Ralph's mother.

Sarah obediently took a step towards the rear of the car but Ralph shook his head.

'Don't bother about the boot. There's plenty of room in the back ...' said Ralph, trailing off as he opened the back door. A smug-looking Bert was sitting there, taking up more than his fair share of the back seat.

Ralph and Sarah looked at each other uneasily.

'Bert's mother rang to ask if I could drive him to the *Officer Cool* filming,' explained Ralph's mother excitedly. 'And we all have passes to get on the set of *Officer Cool*!'

'Whoop-dee-doo,' said Ralph under his breath, sliding in next to Bert.

'Look on the bright side,' said Sarah, getting in after Ralph and closing the door. 'Bert's character might end up getting shot.'

'So how did you get on the show, Bert?' asked Ralph's mother, trying to make light conversation.

'It was very easy,' bragged Bert. 'I just wrote why I liked *Officer Cool* in twenty-five words or less, and I won. Out of thousands of entries.'

'That's very good, Bert,' said Ralph's mother. 'Ralph, did you know about the competition?'

Ralph mumbled something.

'And Sarah, you like *Officer Cool* as well, and you're usually good at winning competitions –' said Ralph's mother.

Sarah leaned forward across Ralph to look squarely at Bert.

'What did you write, exactly, Bert?' challenged Sarah.

'What?' said Bert.

'What were the magic twenty-five words or less that won the competition?' asked Sarah.

'Uh, you know, it was such a long time

ago, I really can't remember,' said Bert, wishing Sarah was sitting right next to him so he could kick or pinch her. Instead he looked out the window.

Sarah glared at the back of Bert's head, noticing how red his neck was turning. Ralph looked curiously from one to the other.

Ralph's mother eyed the children cautiously in the mirror. She put on a bright smile and drove the car through the gateway to Cool TV studios.

'Look. Here we are at Cool TV already,' said Ralph's mother. 'Feeling nervous, Bert?'

'Na. Us professionals don't get nervous,' said Bert.

Sarah poked a finger down her throat as though she was going to vomit.

Ramsey the clapperboy was waiting outside a large, windowless building signposted STUDIO 3.

Bert pointed at him and waved excitedly.

'Look, that's my big brother over there,' said Bert.

'Has he come to watch you, Bert?' asked Ralph's mother.

'Sort of. He's a cameraman on *Officer Cool*,' said Bert.

Sarah drew in her breath sharply and smiled cunningly. Ralph looked at her with interest. He'd seen that smile before, and it meant that Sarah had a plan. Maybe the afternoon wouldn't turn out too badly after all.

As Bert got out of the car, Ramsey tousled Bert's hair.

'Learned your lines, kiddo?' he asked.

'Piece of cake,' said Bert.

Bert shoved a wad of paper at Ralph.

'Read 'em and weep,' said Bert.

Ralph looked at what Bert has just given

him. It was a copy of
the script.

Ralph went to
throw the script in a
rubbish bin he was
passing by, but Sarah
stopped him.

'Hold onto that and read it carefully,' she
warned under her breath.

Ralph looked from the script to Sarah
and back again. He shrugged his shoulders
and walked into the studio, studying the
script carefully.

*

Inside Rick's trailer, Ruby was doing
Penny's make-up.

'Have you learned your lines?' asked
Ruby, grinning.

'I invented the lines. I don't need to learn

them,' said Penny cheekily. 'I just wish I'd realised in time that Bert O'Leary is the horrible bully who sits behind Ralph, so I could have made him come to a sticky end,' she continued ruefully.

'That wouldn't really boost ratings now, would it?' said Ruby. 'Oops, humans coming.'

Penny and Ruby lay down flat as the trailer door opened. Rick and his entourage of wardrobe ladies entered and busied themselves turning Rick into his on-screen persona of *Officer Cool*. When they'd finished, Rick put Penny in his shirt pocket.

'Break a lead!' called Ruby from the make-up bench.

As Rick walked Penny to the studio, for the first time in her showbiz career Penny didn't feel like performing. She had devised the competition hoping that Ralph or

Sarah would win – not Bert, their sworn enemy. But as Rick opened the studio door, Penny saw a familiar figure.

'Ralph?' said Penny, shaking her head and rubbing her eyes in case she was seeing things.

Ralph was sitting on a stool on the opposite side of the studio. His head was in his hands, and he was staring intently at something in his lap. As Rick walked closer she could see that Ralph's eyes were screwed tightly shut and his lips were moving, like he was trying to memorise something for a history test at school. As Rick got closer still, Penny could see that the book in Ralph's lap was the script.

The sound of Rick's footsteps made Ralph look up, and he broke into a grin.

'Hi there, Officer Cool', said Ralph.

'You can call me Rick off-set,' said Rick

chuckling. He looked at Ralph quizzically. 'Hey, haven't we met before? Ralph, isn't it?'

Ralph's mouth dropped open as Rick shook his hand.

Penny squirmed about in Rick's pocket, waiting for Ralph to notice her.

'Learned your lines?' asked Rick.

Before Ralph could reply, or get a good look at Penny, a large shape came between them and knocked Ralph aside.

'Allow me to re-introduce myself. I'm Bert,' said the shape, thrusting its hand out at Rick.

Rick took Bert's hand and shook it dubiously.

'I'm your co-star today,' said Bert pompously.

'Ah,' said Rick, looking past Bert to see if Ralph was okay. 'Well that's … um … excellent.'

 Rick let go of Bert's hand and helped Ralph back up to his feet.

'So are you here for moral support, Ralph?' asked Rick.

'Hmmph,' scoffed Bert. 'This baby was too young to be left at home by himself, so Mummy had to drive him to the studio with us.'

Ralph shot Bert a filthy look.

'You're brothers?' said Rick.

'As if. I'm not related to that piece of scum,' said Bert nastily.

Ralph scowled at Bert, but was too busy rubbing his shoulder to think of a quick response. Rick looked uneasily from one boy to the other.

'That's my real brother over there,' said

Bert, pointing towards Ramsey, who was fiddling with the camera just in front of where Sarah and Mr Wolf were standing.

Sarah jerked her head up.

'Who did you say your brother was, Bert?' asked Sarah so loudly that everyone in the studio, including Mr Wolf, stopped what they were doing and looked at her.

'Gees you're stupid,' snarled Bert. 'You're standing right next to him! The cameraman.'

'You mean … this guy here, who works on the show, is your brother?' asked Sarah incredulously.

'Uh, der. I just said so,' said Bert.

Sarah frowned.

'But I thought cast and crew and their immediate families weren't allowed to enter the competition,' said Sarah, scratching her head for effect.

'So what, Monaghan?' said Bert impatiently.

'So, you should be disqualified,' said Sarah, smiling innocently and turning to Mr Wolf. 'Shouldn't he Mr Wolf?'

Mr Wolf turned red with rage. He didn't like being bossed around at all, especially by an eight-year-old.

'After all, rules are rules,' said Sarah.

Penny, who had never been particularly good at remembering or obeying rules, beamed at Sarah.

Mr Wolf looked angrily at Bert and his brother, then at his watch.

'Technically – Miss Monaghan, is it? – you're right,' said Mr Wolf. 'But we have to shoot this scene right now and at such short notice we won't be able to find another actor –'

'Ralph can do it,' said Sarah.

Ralph looked up, startled.

'I can?' he said.

Mr Wolf looked Ralph up and down.

'Do you know the lines, kid?' he asked.

Ralph nodded eagerly.

Mr Wolf looked from Ralph to Sarah and back again.

'Fine,' he said. 'Shanna, have him ready in five.'

Shanna the make-up lady bustled over to Ralph and poked at him with Ruby. Ralph's face disappeared under a powder cloud of make-up.

Bert shot Sarah an evil look.

'Not just an ugly face, am I?' said Sarah smiling innocently.

'Done!' said Shanna when she'd finished.

When the powder settled, Ralph looked just like himself, only shinier.

'About time,' said Mr Wolf, looking at his watch. 'Places everybody. Three … two … one … Aaaaaaaaaaand … action!'

Ramsey brought Clappers up in front of the camera. This time, instead of dozing or looking scared, Clappers was smiling cunningly.

'Episode 317. Scene 4. Take 1,' said Ramsey. As he slammed the top down on the clapperboard, he accidentally caught his finger in Clappers' teeth. Ramsey let out a muffled yelp of pain.

'That's what you get for cheating, Sunshine,' said Clappers, smiling smugly.

Instead of the usual police headquarters, the set was decorated like a park. Ralph rode a bike from one side to the other, passing a bush along the way. As he passed the bush a masked man jumped out from behind it holding a sack. The masked man tried to pull the sack down over Ralph to kidnap him, but the sack got snagged on something in Ralph's shirt pocket.

'Cut!' cried Mr Wolf.

The 'kidnapper' pulled the sack off Ralph's head. Ralph looked genuinely afraid as Mr Wolf stormed angrily towards him.

Mr Wolf stuck a hand out towards

Ralph's chest and Ralph instinctively pulled away, thinking Mr Wolf was going to slap him. Instead, Mr Wolf reached into Ralph's shirt pocket and pulled out Officer Lead.

'O'Shea. I've found that prop you misplaced,' said Mr Wolf.

Rick patted the shirt pocket where Penny was.

'No. I've got it right here,' said Rick.

Mr Wolf beckoned Rick over. Grudgingly Rick traipsed onto the set where Mr Wolf was holding up Officer Lead.

'Now this is a pencil fit for a police officer,' he said.

'Whereas this –,' Mr Wolf continued, reaching into Rick's pocket and pulling out Penny.

'Hey! That's my pencil!' said Ralph.

Penny was so happy that Ralph recognised her, it brought tears to her eyes.

Mr Wolf passed
Penny to Ralph and
gave Officer Lead
back to Rick.

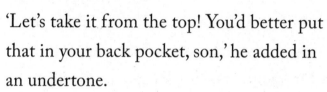

'Everybody got
the right pencil
now?' said Mr Wolf.
'Let's take it from the top! You'd better put
that in your back pocket, son,' he added in
an undertone.

Ralph put Penny in his back pocket. She
snuggled cosily into the fabric of his trousers.

'Aaaaaaaaaaand … action!' said Mr Wolf.

This time Ramsey was holding Clappers
in front of the camera very gingerly.
Ramsey's thumb was bandaged, throbbing
and swollen.

'That showed you, didn't it? You're
not Mr Tough Guy now, are you?' said
Clappers.

'Episode 317. Scene 4. Take 2,' squeaked Ramsey.

Gently, he brought Clappers' teeth together with the tiniest of clicks.

Clappers smiled.

'Now you're learning. That wasn't so hard, was it?' said Clappers.

Although Ralph had only read the script through once, he gave an outstanding performance. He didn't mess up any lines, and the only time they had to stop filming was when one of the cameras ran out of tape.

When filming was over, Ralph, his mother and Sarah said goodbye to Mr Wolf, Rick and Shanna.

Mr Wolf shook Ralph's hand.

'Congratulations, Ralph. That was very well done today. We made the right choice of co-star.' Mr Wolf turned to Sarah. 'Thanks to you, young lady.'

Sarah smiled a knowing smile. In the background Bert scowled.

'Feel free to drop by any time,' said Rick. 'And here's my number if you have any questions about acting,' he continued, passing Ralph an autographed photo.

Ralph's eyes were as round as saucers as he took the photo from Rick.

'Thanks!'

'Ok, kids. Time to go,' said Ralph's mother. She turned to Bert. 'Bert, are you coming with us or going home with your brother?'

Bert just scowled.

'I'll give him a ride,' said Ramsey.

Ralph's mother nodded and walked Sarah and Ralph to the door.

From Ralph's back pocket, Penny peered out at all her friends.

'Bye everyone! Bye Wanda!'

'See you round like a ringlet!' said Wanda.

'Bye Meg!'

Meg made a funny noise as she choked back the tears.

'Bye Ruby!'

Ruby almost disappeared in a cloud of pink powder, she was waving so hard.

'Bye Clappers!'

'Bye Penny. Don't forget to write!' said Clappers.

Penny kept waving all the way out of the studio until the door shut behind her.

Chapter 14

The perfect ending

Since it had been such an eventful afternoon, Ralph's mother decided to pick up Thai take-away on the way home. As a special treat, Ralph's mother let Ralph and Sarah order whatever they wanted.

After their third helping, Ralph and Sarah were too full to eat any more.

'Are you sure you don't want any more?' said Ralph's mother, wondering how all the leftovers were going to fit in the fridge.

'No thanks. I'm full,' said Ralph collapsing in his chair.

'Me too,' said Sarah.

Ralph's mother stood up to clear away the dishes. Sarah got up to help.

'That's okay, Sarah. I'll look after these,' said Ralph's mother. 'You two had better get on with your homework.'

'Aw Mu-um …' said Ralph.

'Come on. You've still got an hour before I promised Sarah's grandmother I'd have her home,' said Ralph's mother.

'But I don't need to do homework,' said Ralph. 'I'm going to be an actor.'

'Oh really?' said Ralph's mother, raising her eyebrows.

'Yeah,' said Ralph proudly.

'Even if you're going to be an actor, you still need to do your homework, Ralph,' said Sarah sternly. 'Remember Rick telling us how he studied hard at school, as well as going to acting classes?'

'Can I start acting classes, Mum?' asked Ralph.

'You can start right now and act like a good little boy, and go and finish your homework,' said Ralph's mother.

Ralph shook his head. There was no way he could argue against both his mother and Sarah.

Ralph's mother took the dishes from the table while Ralph and Sarah pulled out their books to start their homework.

Sarah opened her pencil case and pulled out Polly, and started work straight away.

Some minutes later, after tipping the entire contents of his pencil case out on the table, Ralph still hadn't started.

'What on earth are you doing?' asked

Sarah, when Ralph's fidgeting finally got too much for her.

'I can't find my pencil,' said Ralph sheepishly.

'This one?' said Sarah, reaching into Ralph's back pocket and pulling out Penny.

'Oh. Yeah. Thanks,' said Ralph, flushing.

While Ralph did his homework, Penny waved enthusiastically at Polly and all of Ralph's writing implements who were scattered all over the table.

A half hour later Ralph's mother poked her head out from the kitchen.

'Are you still too full for ice-cream?' she asked Ralph and Sarah.

Ralph and Sarah threw down their pencils and ran into the kitchen.

Once the children had left the room, Penny and Polly hopped up and hugged each other.

Gloop, Mack, Smudge and all Ralph's writing implements gathered around to hug Penny too and ask her questions.

'I'm so glad to be back,' said Penny.

'We're glad to have you back,' said Gloop. 'How did you enjoy being a big TV star?'

'You were right, Gloop,' said Penny. 'It was lots of hard work and I definitely have a lot to learn in school before I go out to seek my fortune in the big, wide world.'

'Why? Wasn't it fun?' asked Smudge.

'It was lots of fun,' said Penny. 'At first. It was all glamorous, and I made some really good friends with Ruby the make-up brush and Clappers the Clapperboard and Meg the Megaphone. But it was a lot of hard work. Long rehearsals, having to study my lines every night. Then when Black Texta showed up and started changing the scripts …'

All the writing implements gasped.

'Did you say … Black Texta?' said Mack incredulously.

'Yes. He's managed to rise from the dead yet again,' said Penny. 'More lives than a cat that evil implement.'

'What happened?'

'How did he get to the TV studio?'

'What did he do?' asked Gloop, Mack and Polly all at once.

Penny explained how

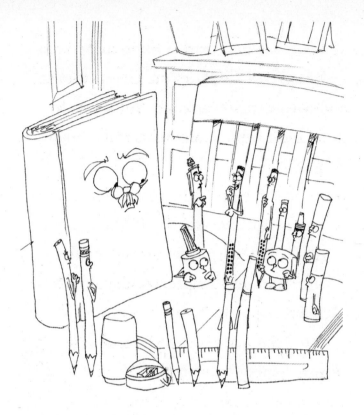

Bert's brother had brought Black Texta
to the studio, and how Black Texta had
deliberately altered the script to make Rick
look bad.

'Rick won't get fired, though, will he?'
asked Polly, wondering how Sarah would
take the news.

'Oh no,' said Penny. 'I put a stop to that.'

'How?' asked Gloop.

'Instead of going head-to-head with him, I fixed the scripts every night,' said Penny, stifling a yawn. She still had a lot of sleep to catch up on.

'So he's still at large?' said Mack, peering carefully into all the corners of Ralph's living-room, as though he expected Black Texta to leap out at any moment.

'Hopefully not for much longer,' said Penny, smiling knowingly. 'I set a trap for him.'

Gloop nodded his approval.

'And?' said Polly hopefully.

'That's the only problem about being home again,' said Penny. 'I won't know whether my plan worked or not …'

Epilogue

Back at the Cool TV studio, Black Texta shimmied down a rope from the air-conditioning duct in Mr Wolf's office. He landed on the desk with barely a sound

– but it was enough to make Cujo's ears
twitch and wake the lamp-beast up.

'Where is it? Where is it?' muttered
Black Texta, fumbling around in the
dark, hunting for the script. He tripped
over something and fell, landing on the
lamp-beast's switch. Mr Wolf's desk was
instantly bathed in light. And sitting right
in the centre of the desk, was the *Officer
Cool* master script.

Black Texta hopped over to the book
and turned a few pages. A low growl made
him stop what he was doing and look
around. There was nobody else in the room.
He shook his head and continued reading
through the script.

'Ha ha ha,' Black Texta laughed evilly.
'Let's just change Rick's line here …'

As Black Texta pulled off his cap, the
lamp-beast snuck up close behind him

and growled a little louder. Black Texta stopped writing and looked around. He still couldn't see anything out of place in the room.

Black Texta bent over and crossed out a line of Rick's dialogue.

'So instead of saying: 'Drop your weapons and put your hands up', Rick will say ...'

As Black Texta bent over the page, the lamp-beast bent over Black Texta until his yellow teeth were only millimetres away. The lamp-beast growled, and Black Texta looked up, just in time to see the lamp-beast's jaws snap tightly around him.